DEVILISH GAME

LINSEY HALL

CARROW

In the last few days, my world had become nothing but bird poo and dust.

My friends and I had been cleaning the newly discovered Shadow Guild tower for three days straight, and we still hadn't made it out of the first room.

"How the *hell* did those pigeons get in here?" I grumbled as I scrubbed at the floor with an ancient mop. "This tower was magically hidden for hundreds of years, and yet those flying rats still managed to get inside and roost."

"I have no idea." My best friend Mac dragged her forearm across her sweaty brow, her hair tied up in a messy knot as she tried to dust the ceiling. "But I must say, this place is turning into some major dead weight."

I heaved a sigh and looked around the main room of the Shadow Guild tower. It was a lot cleaner than it had been, but it had taken us days of scrubbing.

"I've asked every cleaning company in town." Seraphia, the local librarian and one of my new friends, scrubbed vigorously at the windows. "They all refused. They said the place was still too cursed."

I like it. Cordelia, my familiar, grinned at me from her place on the only chair in the room. Somehow, she'd managed to drag the huge wooden thing in there, and she hadn't left it since. *Not close enough to the kebab place though.*

"Your butt is going to become one with that chair soon," I told her. "Why don't you grab a rag and help me out?"

Cordelia gave a strange little chortling laugh and adjusted herself but didn't move to help. Eve, my Fae friend, would be here after her shop closed to help out, and Quinn would swap with Mac when it was time for her shift at the Haunted Hound. There were five of us in the new guild—six, if one included Cordelia, which I didn't since the little freeloader wasn't doing squat to help. But Mac, Quinn, Eve, Seraphia, and I all formed the new Shadow Guild, and we needed to get our tower cleaned up if we were going to be official.

"I can't believe all of this has been hidden so long because of Rasla," Mac said. "That bastard."

Rasla had been a council member hundreds of years ago—one with a serious bone to pick with anyone who was different. Since the Shadow Guild was comprised of all the weirdos in town who didn't fit nicely into any other guild, he'd directed his ire right at it, using a combination of magic and malice to wipe it from the history books.

"I still have no idea why he hated the guild so much," I said. "I want to figure it out, though."

Last week, my friends and I had uncovered the mystery of the ancient guild, solving one of my biggest problems—my guildless status, which would have eventually gotten me kicked out of Guild City. Mac, Eve, Seraphia, and Quinn had all had guilds, but they'd never fit in well. As soon as the Shadow Guild had appeared, it had called to them, a more perfect fit.

Now it was the five of us, trying to make this work. But first, we needed to get it cleaned up so that we officially had a Guild Tower. Whether or not we would live there was still uncertain. Cordelia would mutiny if we moved away from the kebab place, and I liked my new little apartment.

Sighing, I looked at my phone, hoping for a text from Miranda. I hadn't seen Grey since the battle to save the tower. Neither had Miranda, his second in command. We'd never been friendly, but she was as worried as I was. As a vampire and my Cursed Mate, he was doomed to die if he didn't drink me to the death.

Talk about a no-win scenario.

I'd convinced Miranda to text me as soon as he returned, but I'd heard nothing still.

A tentative knock sounded at the door, and I straightened.

Grey?

My heart leapt.

Seraphia, who was closest, leapt down from the deeply inset windowsill and hurried to the door, swinging it open. An older woman with red-rimmed eyes and wild hair stood at the entrance. Even though it was early afternoon, a bathrobe hung off her shoulders.

I stepped forward. "Hello. How can we help you?"

"Are you the new mystery solver in town?" Her voice shook.

"Yes." I gestured her inside. "Come in, please."

Behind me, Cordelia trundled off the chair and pointed to it. *She can sit.*

Sometimes my familiar managed to pull some manners out of the dumpster. I gestured to the chair. "Please, sit. I'm sorry. We don't have any refreshments we can offer you."

"I couldn't drink or eat if I tried." Her voice was so thin it seemed like it would break. She ignored the chair and came to me, gripping my arms tight. "My baby has been stolen. My Katine—just nineteen. She was taken right out of her bed late last night."

I gasped. "Kidnapped?"

The woman nodded her head, her teary eyes desperate and her grip viselike. "I heard a bit of noise but thought nothing of it. Then a few minutes later—a scream, short and fierce."

The guilt in her voice sounded heavy enough to drag her to the bottom of the Pacific. "Did you see anything?"

Mac, Seraphia, and Cordelia all gathered around, concern vibrating off them.

"I ran to the window." The woman's voice nearly broke, but she stiffened her spine. "A man—perhaps a demon—was dragging her through the back garden, right into a portal he made with a transport charm."

Oh, shit. This was so much worse than a normal kidnapping case. In the human world, you had twenty-four hours to solve the case before your chances plummeted. In the magical world, with portals and transport charms, you had minutes.

They could be anywhere by now. I could see the thought reflected in my friends' eyes, but none of us spoke it aloud.

"You didn't go to the police?" I asked.

"I did. I've just come from there. But they're slow. And I've heard what you've done for Guild City. If you can save so many, surely you can save Katine."

Oh God, that was a lot of pressure. But I had to try.

"What did the kidnapper look like? Did he leave anything behind?"

I tightened my hands into fists, wishing that my power didn't require something to touch.

"He looked human for the most part, but he had terrible red eyes. Evil eyes." She bared her teeth in a snarl, as if she could reach through her memories and strangle the kidnapper. "He was tall—dreadfully so. Two meters if he was an inch. And he wore a dark cloak that concealed almost all of him except a shock of dark hair and the red eyes. Like blood, they were."

I looked at Seraphia and Mac. "Have you ever heard of anyone like that?"

They shook their heads.

I looked back at the woman. "And you have nothing of his? Nothing from the scene?"

"I can go search again. I didn't spend long before I went to the police. But they...." She shook her head, clearly irritated. "They're working on it, but too slowly."

"I can try." I really needed something to touch, though. I held out my hand, palm up. "May I touch you?"

She frowned. "I suppose so."

"Thank you. My gift relies on touch."

She thrust out her hand. "Anything for Katine."

Gently, I laid my palm on hers, trying to corral my magic into doing my bidding. *Show me what she saw.*

An image blasted into my mind. A young woman,

pale and terrified, was being dragged backward by a cloaked figure with brilliant red eyes. She screamed, fighting his grip, but he was too strong. He slammed a transport charm to the ground, and a poof of orange smoke burst up next to them. He dragged Katine into it, and the vision ended. I shuddered, withdrawing my hand from the woman's.

"The portal was orange. Is that strange?" I'd only been in the magical world a short while, but all the transport charm portals I'd seen had been silver gray.

"That is strange," Mac said. "There could be some residue left behind if you're lucky."

"Could Eve track that?" My Fae friend was a potion master. In this strange, magical world, she was a combination of forensics and weaponry.

"Maybe," Mac said.

"Do you want me to take you?" the woman said. "It hasn't rained yet, and the garden is shaded from the sun."

"All right."

"Come." She turned, her bathrobe flapping.

"Wait, I don't know your name," I said.

"Oh, of course." She turned back, eyes weary and face drawn. "I'm Martha Templeton. Mother of Katine Templeton."

"I'm Carrow Burton, Martha." My phone buzzed in my pocket, making me jump. I pulled it out, my heart leaping when I saw the two little words from Miranda.

.   .   .

He's back.

Mac's eyes zeroed in on my face, knowledge sparking in her gaze. "I'll go to Martha's and get a sample if there is one. You go see what's going on there."

I hated not going with Martha, but for all I knew, Grey was at death's door. The curse had an unknown time frame, but soon it would drag him to hell. He already wasn't healing normally, his immortality draining away because of our Cursed Mate bond. I'd appeared in his life, and now he was fated to die.

I suppressed the shudder and nodded. Mac could get the sample and, if I needed to, I could visit the site as soon as I'd seen Grey. "Thank you, Mac."

"No problem."

"If you need anything from the library, just let me know," Seraphia said.

"The library?" Skepticism sounded in Martha's voice.

"You never know what secrets can be revealed by research," Seraphia said.

Martha nodded, but the skepticism didn't fade from her eyes.

We split up, Martha taking Mac to her home while I raced through the streets to Grey's tower. It was a quiet afternoon, the shops doing a slow business as people ambled around the historic streets browsing for magical objects. Normally, I'd window shop while walking down the ancient roads, but not today.

I had eyes only for Grey's tower, and I darted through the sparse crowd, reaching his headquarters in record time.

The tall tower loomed against the steel gray sky, the black stone ominous in the hazy light. Two massive shifter guards stood outside the doors. Depending on how you looked at it, they were bouncers for his club or bodyguards for the most powerful criminal kingpin in Guild City.

Also known as my Cursed Mate.

How my life had taken this turn so quickly, I'd never know. One day I was a poor wannabe detective living in a shitty flat in a bad part of London, no friends and no prospects besides the raccoon who lived in the alley outside my place.

Now, I was a magical sleuth living in an enchanted, medieval city—full of the modern conveniences, of course—with friends and a man who was going to break my heart if we didn't fix this Cursed Mate tragedy.

The only thing that had remained the same was the raccoon, and even she was vastly different than I'd expected.

Without hesitating, I strode up to the large double

doors. The bouncers inclined their heads, recognizing me, and opened the doors.

"Thanks, guys." I hurried in, spotting Miranda standing at the tall podium in the foyer. It was the only piece of furniture in the room, and she the only person.

Miranda guarded Grey's kingdom from this room, funneling people to his club or to his office, depending. As usual, she was dressed in a trim pencil skirt and buttoned up blouse, her hair in a severe knot. She was beautiful and competent, as cold and sharp as a knife.

Usually, anyway. At the moment, she looked worried. I'd never seen her with a creased brow and shadowed eyes, but right now, she vibrated with concern. Her gaze landed on me. "He's in his flat."

I nodded and turned down the appropriate hall. Normally she would escort me, but she stayed where she was. It took a minute to navigate my way to the back of the tower and, as I went, my heart began to pound louder and louder.

Finally, I reached his doors and knocked.

Please be okay.

2

CARROW

The door swung open, revealing Grey, pale and skinnier than I'd last seen him, with shadows under his eyes and sharper cheekbones that made his full lips look even more sinful.

Worry twisted in my chest. "You look like hell."

"And you look like heaven." A worried frown flashed in his eyes. "I shouldn't have said that."

"I like it." I entered, reaching up to cup his cheek.

He moved back before I could make contact and hurt flickered inside me. "You don't want me to touch you?"

"It's not wise."

I nodded, knowing he was probably right. Last week,

we'd had the best night of my life. But we couldn't do that again. Not with the way our future was shaping up.

Worry twisted my heart as I entered his beautiful flat. Austere, yet gorgeous, the space had a high ceiling and an enormous wall of windows that looked out on a tormented, wave-capped beach. It was magic, of course, but I couldn't help but think that the tumultuous beach represented the state of Grey's soul or . . . whatever.

He was a desperate mess, like I was.

I turned to him, taking in the broad shoulders that were still capped with heavy muscle despite the weight loss. His suit still fit perfectly, of course. It should be impossible. "Where have you been?"

"Worried?"

"Yes."

The corner of his mouth tugged up in the smallest smile. "Don't be. I've found a solution to our problem."

"Is that why you look like hell?"

"It wasn't easy, true. But it's also just the nature of the curse. Hell is calling my name."

I couldn't believe it. He was a good person. True, he had a terrible past and was involved in some seriously shady dealings, but he was fundamentally good. But even if heaven called his name, that still wasn't a place I could go. Not yet.

If ever.

I shook the thought away. "What is the solution? Will it save you?"

"I believe so. I've found a spell and a sorceress in town who can break our Cursed Mate bond."

Hope flared. "So we won't be cursed anymore?"

"We won't be mates."

Disappointment surged, but I tamped it down. If this was the only way, then . . . of course I'd do it. I wasn't even sure I *believed* in fated mates anyway. It wasn't like I'd been born to this world and grown up with it.

"If we're not mates, then we can't be cursed," I said. "That's how it works?"

"Precisely."

"Who is it? Can they do it now?" As much as I didn't want to break the bond, Grey looked like hell. He needed all the help we could get, and he needed it soon.

"They can. Immediately. It won't take long."

Mac was on the trail of the kidnappings. I had to take the time for this. "Let's go."

He nodded, his gaze lingering on me for a moment. His lips parted, as if he wanted to say something, but no words came out. I swallowed hard and moved toward the door. "Come on. No time to waste."

"Of course." He followed me out of his flat, and I couldn't believe we were already on our way. How was this happening so damned fast?

I looked back at him, catching sight of the exhaustion in his eyes.

This only feels fast to me.

"You've been going nonstop since we parted, haven't you?" I asked. "Looking for a cure."

He nodded.

I reached for his hand and squeezed. "I'm glad you found one."

He squeezed back, just briefly, then dropped the small embrace. Hurt pierced me, and I tried to shove it away. He was clearly ready to be rid of me and this bond. After the night we'd spent together, though...

It was hard to believe.

Well, believe it, cookie. Life is full of disappointments.

"Where are we going?" I asked, wanting to get my mind off the miserable train of thought.

"To Hellebore Alley, not far from my tower. There's a blood sorceress called Cyrenthia who can help us."

"Blood sorceress?"

"A magic that teeters on the edge of dark. The key ingredient to her magic is blood. Taken willingly, her magic falls on the right side of the law. Taken unwillingly..."

"Dark magic."

"Precisely." He nodded at Miranda as we passed, and she watched him with steely eyes. The worry that I'd seen on her face earlier was gone, hidden no doubt when he was around.

Grey led me out into the square in front of his tower. The clouds had grown even more ominous, dropping lower in the sky, and taking on the shade of gunmetal. It was almost as if the weather agreed that sad shit was about to happen.

Of course I wanted to fix Grey. I'd cut open my vein right away and let the blood sorceress take whatever she wanted. But breaking our bond ...

It felt like breaking the thing that was growing between us, and I was definitely conflicted about that. I shouldn't fall for the tortured, ancient vampire, but I was beginning to teeter at the edge. And I was liking it.

"How is your guild tower coming along?" he asked.

His words dragged me to the present, and I looked up at him. "Fine. We're getting there, but its slow."

"Good. I'm glad to hear it's working out." He approached an alley that smelled vaguely foul. Nothing overtly terrible—more like a swamp than a dumpster— but it wasn't pleasant.

He turned down the alley, and I followed, spotting the sign on the brick wall at the corner. *Hellebore Alley.*

The air felt thicker, as if it were coated with smog. It was darker as well, the clouds hovering around the roofs of the buildings. The alley was so narrow that Grey and I had to walk shoulder to shoulder. On either side of the little road, the buildings rose three stories high.

In the style of Tudor buildings, the upper floors jutted out over the lower ones, the overhang creating a tunnel effect. The dark wooden beams surrounded gunmetal gray plaster. It had once been white, the usual color, but soot appeared to have coated the surface.

Grey caught me looking. "That's the stain of dark magic. The top floors are flats. Rent is cheap in this part of town."

No surprise. The letting advert would say something like *Charming hovel in a perpetually gloomy part of town. Sun never seen.*

The windows of the upper floors were all shuttered, either by wood or curtains, as if the inhabitants were constantly walking around in their knickers and couldn't risk being spotted by the people in the windows across the road.

Given the dark magic stink in the air, however, I had a feeling that it wasn't nakedness that kept the windows covered.

The contents of the shops were nothing like those on the other streets. Sure, they had the same magical aura that made the contents of the windows move around, but the contents . . .

I shuddered.

One window was full of weapons. Normally, I'd be entranced. I loved a good blade. But these were different. They were the sharpest, evilest looking daggers I'd ever seen. Serrated teeth and double pronged. In the window, they stabbed at the air, darting around with an aggression that was so different from the elegant, fanciful movements of weapons in the shop windows in the rest of Guild City.

Worse, the blades were speckled with a rusty brownish-red.

"Is that blood on the blades?" I asked.

"I would think so, yes."

I shivered and looked toward the next shop. Hundreds of potion vials sat on the shelves, vibrating with a low hum that radiated through the glass, making a shudder run through me. My stomach turned, and I pressed a hand to it.

"Breathe through your mouth," Grey said. "It helps."

"Why does it feel like that?" I shot the vials another look, not liking the way the neon contents made my eyes burn just from looking at them.

"The nature of the potions. They're all exceedingly unpleasant."

My gaze riveted to the next shop window, which made the 'unpleasant' potions look like a sunny day in the park. It was by far the worst display I'd ever seen. Possibly the worst *thing* I'd ever seen.

Severed body parts floated in the air, all of them withered and wrinkled. Claws and talons tipped the hands, and the organs were unlike any I'd ever seen in diagrams or at the coroner's office.

"What *is* that place?" I whispered, my stomach turning.

"Demon body parts emporium. They're used in spells."

I shook my head, horrified. "I don't care if demons

are the personification of evil and their souls wake back up in their hells, that seems wrong."

"I must say that I agree." He walked a bit faster, putting himself between me and the shops so that I couldn't easily see what was inside.

"Thanks. I've definitely seen enough." I kept my gaze glued on the cobblestone walkway that gleamed gold and dark beneath the streetlamps that burned even in daylight. The stones looked wet, though it hadn't rained recently. In fact, this whole place appeared damp.

"We're nearly there," he said.

"Thank fates. I'm surprised the Council lets a place like this exist."

"They toe the line between legal and illegal. And there are some bribes involved."

"Do you facilitate any of those?"

"For the blood sorceress, yes. For places like the demon body parts emporium ... definitely not."

"Why does she live over here if she is a member of the Sorcerer's Guild? I thought they liked to stick together—loyalty and all that." The sorcerers were generally bastards to outsiders, but they were a fiercely loyal bunch amongst themselves. I quite admired it, actually.

"She's not a member of that guild. Not formally, at least."

"What do you mean?"

"She's a member in the same way that I'm a member

of the Vampire Guild. She pays dues so that the Sorcer-er's Guild will claim her, and the Council leaves her alone. But she isn't involved with them in any way."

"That's possible? Could I have done that if the Shadow Guild hadn't appeared?"

"It requires money and connections, but yes."

"Oh. I don't have those."

He looked down at me. "Yes, you do."

"Connections, maybe." I nudged his shoulder. He was pretty much the most powerful connection one could have in Guild City, albeit an unorthodox one. "But money? No."

"I do."

"You'd have used it for me?" Surprise surged inside me.

A perplexed look flickered in his eyes. "I don't see how that is a question. Of course I would have."

Our bond might be broken in a short while, magi-cally torn asunder, but how could I not fall for a guy like this? He *always* had my back.

"But it was a last resort," he said. "It's a careful balance to be outside of a guild, and always more dangerous. You're safer as a true member. That was always the goal."

"And now I am." I had my ragtag guild—tiny, but fierce.

Grey stopped in front of a dark red door. It was ornately carved with roses and vines. The thorns looked deadly sharp and dripped a dark red liquid that drew my gaze. "Is that blood?"

"The blood of everyone who has requested services. Including ours." He raised a hand and pierced his thumb on a thorn that wasn't dripping. Dark blood welled, and he removed his hand. The gleaming droplet hung suspended, not falling.

I did the same, wincing slightly at the little pinch of pain. When I removed my hand, my blood hung immobile as well. Magic swirled around the door, a dark mist that traveled up the front of the three-story building. It was Tudor, like the rest, but the wooden beams surrounded red plaster instead of the usual grayish white, giving the place an ominous feel.

A moment later, a tiny hatch in the main door opened. It was about waist level, and a withered hand appeared, holding a golden goblet. Black liquid swirled within, and ornate golden rings decorated the fingers on the hand. Dark red talons tipped each withered finger, and I flashed Grey a startled look.

"What?" I mouthed.

"You are worthy." The creaky voice intoned from behind the door, cutting off any response he might have given. "Now make your offering."

Grey raised his thumb to his mouth and pierced with a fang, then held his hand over the cup. The wound bled freely, and he allowed a thin stream to drip into the cup.

When he finished, I raised my hand, assuming I had to go, too.

He shook his head, and I lowered my hand.

"Her, too," the voice said.

"It is unnecessary," he said. "I have made the offering."

"Two wish for services, two will make the offering." The voice was firm despite its obvious age and the weakness of the speaker. The withered hand trembled as it held the glass.

"It's fine." I raised my hand and drew my own small knife, cutting my finger, feeling the pain pinch as the blood welled. I let it pour over the cup, dripping into the dark liquid. Only a few drops had fallen when Grey gripped my arm and withdrew it. "That's enough."

I pressed my thumb to the cut, staunching the flow.

The hand withdrew, and the little door slammed shut. A few moments passed, and I looked up at Grey, catching sight of something unidentifiable in his eyes. "What?"

"Would that I could heal you." There was a slight wistfulness to his voice.

How the *hell* was I supposed to not fall for a guy like this?

Impossible.

"You'll be better soon enough, your healing abilities returned." I stared at the closed door, waiting. "What's happening?"

"I'm not sure you want to know."

"I do."

Before he could answer, the main door creaked open, revealing a stunningly beautiful woman. Brilliant red hair fell down her back, and blinding green eyes glittered with life. She wore a black robe trimmed in what looked like diamonds, and it swayed around her as if blown by an impossible wind that no one else could feel.

I blinked, surprised.

Where had the crone gone? There was no way she was the same person who had stuck the goblet out of the tiny hatch.

And yet, she was holding it. Her fingers were tipped with scarlet nails and the same golden rings glinted on her fingers. Even her lips were gleaming a vibrant red. At first, I'd taken it to be lipstick.

But no, it was blood.

My blood.

This woman had drunk our blood and grown young again.

Wow.

And *yuck.*

"Devil." Her voice hummed seductively low, nothing like the voice that had filtered through the door. "So pleased to see you again."

"Cyrenthia." His voice was devoid of emotion. "May we enter?"

"But of course. I have everything prepared, as you requested. We just need to call upon my colleague, and we'll be ready to start."

"Colleague?" he asked.

"Mordaca of Darklane. This requires powerful magic." Her gaze turned to me. "This is the one?"

"I'm Carrow Burton." I inclined my head in greeting, not extending my hand.

"Hmm." Her lips pursed, and it was clear she wasn't impressed.

I suppressed a scowl. We needed her. And maybe she was being miserable because she had a thing for Grey. Why wouldn't she?

"Come." She turned and strode down the short, empty hall, entering a room at the back.

We followed, stepping into a surprisingly modern space. The walls had been plastered smooth and decorated with dark glass mirrors. They shimmered with an eerie light, appearing full of smoke. My reflection was dimmed, just a shadow of myself, and I drew my gaze away, not liking the hollow feeling that rose in my chest when I looked into them.

The furniture was low and sleek, dark leather and extremely uncomfortable looking. A huge table was covered in all manner of cauldrons, tiny metal tools, and vials of ingredients. Shelves of similar items lined one wall, and a black marble fireplace flickered with bright orange fire.

"Just a moment." Cyrenthia walked toward one of the mirrors and knocked, shouting, "Mordaca! Come on, I need you."

A voice grumbled from the other side. "Your timing is foul, Cyrenthia."

Cyrenthia grinned widely, as if the words pleased her. She glanced back over her shoulder. "Mordaca keeps late hours."

A moment later, the shadowy image of a woman appeared in the mirror. She stepped through, one bare leg appearing first through the glass. A black stiletto heel landed gracefully on the ground, and the rest of the woman followed.

She wore a deeply cut black dress that revealed miles of cleavage. It was cut high on her leg, falling in waves behind her. A pound of black eye makeup swept out from her eyes, looking like a mask that Cordelia would envy. Her hair was piled high on her head in a bouffant, and her entire aesthetic looked a hell of a lot like Elvira, Mistress of the Dark.

I looked between her and Cyrenthia. They were like two sides of the same crazy coin. What the hell were they going to do to us?

3

GREY

Cyrenthia and Mordaca turned toward us, both grinning widely. It was an eerie effect, blood lust gleaming in their eyes.

"Thank you for transferring the money so quickly," Mordaca said. "Shall we get started?"

I inclined my head. The money had been the least of it. The journey to find this spell had taken me three miserable days, every step of it shadowed with doubt.

The truth of the matter was . . . I didn't want to be parted from Carrow. Breaking our bond made my heart shrivel inside my chest into a shape even smaller than it had been before.

Yet, it was the only way.

I didn't want to be dragged to hell. And I didn't want to return to the blood lust I'd felt as a turned vampire. All my desperate research suggested that as my strength waned and the grip of hell became stronger, my desire to feed on her would grow—possibly to the point that I couldn't control it. I could still remember the early days, when I'd been nothing but a rabid mess of hunger, rampaging across Transylvania, more animal than man.

No.

No matter what it cost, I would not subject Carrow to that.

She deserved better than me, anyway. This would allow her to find it.

"Well?" Cyrenthia raised a brow, and I jerked slightly, realizing that they were waiting for my attention.

"Apologies." I was never caught daydreaming—yet here I was.

This needed to happen fast.

"What do you need from us?" I asked.

"A bit of your blood." Cyrenthia looked down at the ancient scroll I'd retrieved for her. "We'll take care of the rest."

Carrow was already drawing her dagger from her pocket. Mordaca brought over an onyx bowl, and Cyrenthia hurried to the wall of shelves and began to collect various tiny vials of liquid and powder. While Carrow cut into her vein, I pierced my wrist with my fangs. We both allowed a thin stream of liquid to drip into the bowl that Mordaca held. Cyrenthia worked at the table, combining various ingredients in a larger cauldron.

Mordaca joined her, adding our blood to the mix. She watched Cyrenthia work, dark brows raised and scarlet lips pursed.

"Quit judging," Cyrenthia said.

"Wouldn't dream of it." Mordaca sounded sincere, but her eyes sparkled with laughter. She bit her lip, clearly wanting to comment on Cyrenthia's technique.

"It's ready for you." Cyrenthia stepped back from the cauldron.

Mordaca stepped up, raising her hand over the cauldron. She sliced her thumb with one of her long, pointed nails, shaking her hand a bit so that her blood could pour into the cauldron. She held her hand carefully, not allowing us to see the blood itself, but there was something strange about it. My vampire senses picked up on it, but I couldn't identify where the oddness came from. Cyrenthia added her blood next.

Carrow leaned close and murmured. "Why do they add their blood?"

"There is magic in their blood. It's what makes the spell work, and it's why we needed Mordaca. She's one of the most powerful blood sorceresses in the world."

"Yet she doesn't live here?"

"She lives in Magic's Bend, Oregon. One of the largest all-magical cities in America."

Cyrenthia finished contributing her blood, then picked up the cauldron and carried it to the fire. Instead of hooking the vessel onto the hanger over the flames so that it could heat, she dumped the entire contents onto the flames.

As it hissed and sizzled, she and Mordaca began to chant ancient words in a language long dead. Their voices rose in a low, vibrating hum as magic began to spark in the air. The flames roared higher, a dark smoke coalescing over them.

The smoke condensed, drawing in on itself until it was black as midnight. It grew heavy, the cloud lowering over the flames.

"It's ready." Cyrenthia held the now empty cauldron over the flames, right beneath the cloud of heavy black smoke. The smoke liquefied itself, pouring back into the cauldron.

"Wow." Carrow whistled low. "I didn't realize physics could work like that."

"Magic, darling. Not physics." Mordaca smiled. "I think it is time I took my leave. My beauty sleep calls me."

It was mid-morning in Oregon by now, but that was Mordaca.

She strolled to the mirror. Before stepping in, she threw a glance over her shoulder. "Be careful what you wish for. You may find that the results are not what you desire."

A scowl crept across my face. Damned cryptic sorcerers. Of course I didn't wish for these results, but they were necessary.

With a grin, she stepped back through the mirror and disappeared.

Cyrenthia brought the cauldron to us, along with two silver ladles. "Now, all you must do is drink."

Carrow's gaze flicked to mine. "Is it really that easy to fix all of this?"

"Easy?" Cyrenthia scoffed. "Do you see how hellish he looks? He walked into the bowels of the place itself to get this spell, and nothing about my magic is easy. Not to mention, the magic of your bond is powerful. You'll feel it when it is gone, and you will mourn."

"I apologize." Her gaze caught mine, worry flickering in her eyes. "Are we doing this now?"

"Yes." Memories of the night last week flashed in my mind. It had been the best night of my life. Not solely because of the act, but because of how it *felt*.

Those feelings would be lost now. After a drought of emotion for hundreds of years, I should be used to that state. Hell, I should welcome it back. Life was simpler and easier that way, certainly.

Yet, I dreaded it.

Fate seemed to be pulling at my arm as I raised it to take the ladle, trying to drag me backward. I resisted, taking the utensil. Carrow took hers as well.

"Drink at the same time," Cyrenthia said.

I nodded, dipping my ladle and retrieving some of the potion. Carrow grimaced and did the same.

"Don't be a ninny," Cyrenthia said. "It's no big deal to drink a little blood."

"Frankly, that sounds insane," Carrow said. "But I'm not from your world, so I'm going to trust you."

"You'd better." Cyrenthia scowled.

Carrow almost scowled back—her nose wrinkled just slightly, and her eyes narrowed—but she smoothed her features and nodded. I could feel how on edge she was. The tension vibrated off her.

Did she not want to break the bond?

Of course she did. That was ridiculous.

But maybe . . . just maybe . . . she felt the tiniest bit of regret for what might have been. It all but swallowed me alive.

"Now?" I asked, forcing myself toward the task.

"Now." She raised her ladle.

We drank, maintaining eye contact. The potion was sweet and sour at the same time, and I swore I could taste the faintest hint of Carrow's blood. The beast roared inside, me, but I forced it back, aided by the potion that raced through my body.

Magic sparked along every nerve ending, shooting through muscle and bone. When it happened, I felt it, so strong and fierce.

The bond broke, like a great tree snapping in the middle and tumbling to the ground. Loss surged through me, followed by despair.

I stiffened, clenching my jaw.

I must get ahold of myself.

This kind of reaction was unacceptable.

But the bond was broken. I could feel it. The invisible threads of fate that had bound us together were severed, and their absence was like a lost limb.

Carrow's eyes flickered, but it was impossible to read them. She raised a hand toward my face, and I nearly leaned into her touch. Before she made contact, she closed her fist and lowered her hand. "You look better."

I caught sight of my reflection in one of the mirrors, and the change was obvious. The weight that I'd lost had returned, and I looked like myself again.

Cyrenthia frowned at us, her gaze flicking back and forth.

"What?" I asked.

"Your bond . . . it is severed, but . . . You must be careful. Do not spend much time together. You must not fall for each other, or I can't guarantee that fate won't reassert itself."

It was like a punch to the gut.

Of course we couldn't be around each other. I shouldn't even assume that Carrow would want that. But . . .

To face it.

My future looked bleak without her, an endless dark tunnel that pressed in on me.

"Sure." Carrow smiled. "Thank you for the help."

Cyrenthia nodded, her gaze still glued on us. It burned.

"Come." I nodded my thanks to Cyrenthia and turned. "We should go."

"There's no *we* any longer," Cyrenthia said.

Of course. I turned back to Carrow, unable to believe it all ended here, in a shite part of town with a blood sorceress watching our corpses with the avarice of a vulture. "Goodbye, Carrow."

She blinked, looking almost surprised, then hurried after me out of the shop.

~

Carrow

Grey moved quickly out of Cyrenthia's place, and I had to hustle to keep up. My chest felt so . . .strange.

I'd felt the bond break. It had snapped like a twig, leaving me feeling empty and hollow. Cyrenthia said I would feel its absence, and that I would mourn.

She was right.

Yet, Grey wasn't a stranger to me. I still cared. True, the insane pull toward him that I'd been feeling had vanished. That heavy hand of fate.

But I still felt for him—how could I not?

We could just never be together, or the curse might return. Pain pierced my heart.

Yet he was so much healthier looking now. This had been worth it. We'd had no other choice.

I caught up with him about halfway down the alley, squeezing alongside him. He looked down, surprised. "We shouldn't spend time together."

"I-I know." I shook my head. "I'm sorry. I risk your life by pushing."

He spun toward me, his entire form vibrating with suppressed emotion. "It's not that. You shouldn't be so confident in my strength."

"You would never hurt me." I'd tried to get him to take my blood when I'd lain dying, and he'd refused. "You would never do what fate compels you to."

"*I* wouldn't. But there is a beast inside me, Carrow. The vampire within is not always controlled by the man. As my strength waned these last days, the beast fought to rise, as it had in the past. You weren't there then, but when the beast gains control and is driven by blood lust, there is no fighting it. I can't guarantee that I would not turn on you."

He loomed over me, and my back pressed against the wall. All around, the tall buildings rose high, over-hanging the street and creating a tunnel. I should have been afraid, but I couldn't be.

"You wouldn't hurt me." I *knew* it. Just like I knew that the alternative to hurting me was his death. Cyrenthia was right. We couldn't be around each other. We couldn't fall for each other. "I never should have followed you. I'm sorry."

He drew in an unsteady breath and stepped backward, composing himself. "I apologize for losing my temper."

I nodded and, together, we left the alley in silence. As soon as we stepped onto the brighter main street, a woman appeared in front of us.

Mary, my witch friend. Her magenta eyes were wild, and her pink hair messy. She wore a glittery silver dress that was more suited to midnight than the middle of the day, but the witches marched to the beat of their own drummer.

"Hi, Mary."

"Carrow." Her tone was frantic. "You need to help me. Beth has been taken."

"Beth?" I hadn't seen the other witch in a few days. "Taken? What do you mean?"

"She was taken right off the street." Her voice shook. "We're looking for her, of course, but nothing is working. It's just been so . . . so . . ."

Her words trailed off, and her wild eyes searched the alley around us.

"Come here. Let's sit down." She *really* needed a seat. So did I. Beth was one of my friends. Worry made my heart race. I gestured for her to follow me toward a small garden that was nestled between two buildings across the street. A bench beckoned.

All around the bench, roses climbed up the wall of the tiny garden. A little fountain burbled in front of it and, as we sat on the bench, dozens of roses unfurled, opening to the late-afternoon sun. Faerie lights sparkled inside of them, glowing with magic as their heavenly scent filled the air.

Grey followed, his brow creased. He hovered at the entrance to the garden, watching us with concern. He really should have been on his way back to his place, but I didn't have the heart to tell him to scram. Not like I could control his actions anyway. And he knew what was at stake.

"Tell me what's wrong." I searched her frantic eyes.

Mary drew in a shuddering breath. "Beth was abducted. The whole guild is trying to find her, but we need help."

"Abducted?" No. Not Beth. Fear pierced me, cold and horrible. And two in the same night? And both on my doorstep? "From where? By whom?"

"We were out partying. It was late, and we were walking home. Beth thought she might be sick, so she dipped into Hangman's Alley. She was only there a moment when a bloke with red eyes nabbed her. Dragged her right through an orange portal."

Holy crap.

Serial kidnappings.

There was no way the two were unrelated. Not with the red eyes and orange portal.

Grey leaned forward from his spot by the garden entrance. "Red eyes, you say?"

Mary nodded frantically. "Unlike anything I've ever seen. They burned like fire."

Recognition flashed in Grey's eyes.

"You know something about this?" I asked, hope flaring.

Mary cringed back, as if recognizing the Devil of Darkvale for the first time. Her voice was tremulous when she said, "*You.*"

"Not I, if that's what you're implying," Grey said. "I did not kidnap your friend. It is not quite the business I am in."

Her pale face did not regain any color, and it reminded me of Grey's reputation around town. I'd gotten to know him well enough that I didn't think much of it any longer, but he was still the most powerful kingpin in all of Guild City. Also, the most feared.

I turned back to Mary. "Is there anything else you can tell me about the abduction? Anything left at the scene, perhaps?"

"No, I checked. Then the whole guild checked just for good measure. Not even a shard of the transport charm on the ground."

"They vaporize when used," Grey said.

"Right." Mary nodded. "There was nothing. Beth

was there one moment and gone the next."

I leaned back against the bench, my mind racing. I needed leads. More than just red eyes and orange portals. There was already a lot at stake, but with Beth also

abducted . . .

This had become so much more important.

My gaze flicked to Grey, who was clearly chewing on something inside his mind. He recognized something about this.

I rubbed Mary's shoulder. "Beth wasn't the only one abducted last night, and I'm already trying to find who's responsible. What are you and the guild doing?"

"Searching spells, mostly. We're scrying to try to find her, but it's not working."

"Keep it up," I said. "Anything helps. And I'm going to start looking for Beth immediately."

"Thank you, Carrow." She hugged me tight. "I knew you would."

"Of course. Beth's my friend."

Mary stood, still shaking, and disappeared down the street.

Grey moved aside so she could leave the garden but didn't come to sit next to me. I stood, staring at him. "What do you know?"

"I know who's responsible for the kidnappings—or at least, whose goons did the dirty work."

Elation jumped. "Tell me!"

"Not here." His gaze flicked to the wall of roses behind me.

I looked back at the gorgeous flowers, my skin prickling with wariness. *The walls have eyes.* The old saying came to mind, and I rose. "Come on. We'll go back to my place. I'm waiting for Mac to come back from the other crime scene."

He nodded, and together we strode down the street toward my flat. We walked in silence, which was for the best.

About halfway to my flat, I said, "We're not far from Hangman's Alley, are we?"

"Only a couple streets over."

"Let's check it out real quick. Maybe I'll get something." I cut through the streets, grateful for my sense of direction. I didn't know the entire town yet, but I knew a lot of it, especially the part around my flat.

Hangman's Alley was a tiny little thing, an empty alley devoid of shops or bins. I definitely wasn't surprised that it was frequently used as an impromptu loo by drunken kids.

We reached it a moment later, and I slipped into the cool, dark space. It was only a few feet wide, so narrow that it seemed pointless. And, of course, it smelled of wee.

I held my nose and ran my hands along the stone wall.

Please, please show me something.

4

CARROW

The alley wall was rough under my fingertips as I used my magic to try to read the stones.

What happened here last night? Who abducted Beth?

Red exploded in my mind, brilliant and violent, the color so blinding that it made my brain ache. Amongst the swirling bright red fog in my mind, a figure stood. I couldn't see them clearly, but they were there. The power that radiated off the figure nearly sent me to my knees.

Screams of pain and the clash of steel sounded in my head, bringing with it the scent of mud and blood.

War.

A connection formed, something fierce and strong that pulled me toward the figure.

"Come to me." The voice was deep and low in my head, blasting through me. Violence made audible.

Repulsion filled me.

I couldn't go to this figure. Never. It would be the death of me. The death of so many.

Suddenly, the redness faded. Calm descended, white and pure. There was still a figure hidden amongst the mist, but they remained invisible.

"You must resist." The voice was no longer terrifying. Instead, it was desperate. "You must stop this."

What the hell was going on?

Two strong hands appeared on my shoulders, pulling me back. The connection broke. I gasped, stumbling against Grey's strong chest. He clutched me close, keeping me upright.

"What happened?" he asked.

I pulled away, mourning the loss of the connection, and turned to him. "I don't know. I just had the strangest vision. Like I was standing with someone."

"You went totally still, like you went somewhere else."

I turned back to the wall. "Maybe I did."

His hand lightly touched my shoulder. "Your magic has grown."

I shivered, feeling it race through me. Whatever had just happened had been different than the other times I'd used my skills. But why? My power was growing in such a weird, convoluted way. There was no pattern.

I looked at Grey. "I don't know what I just saw, but it has to do with the kidnappings."

"And it made your power grow?"

I shivered, worried. "I don't know."

"But this is linked to you, somehow."

"I don't know." My throat felt tight. "It was all so fast. It's all just feelings. How am I supposed to learn anything from that?"

"Powerful magic follows no rhyme or reason, somehow."

The words were no comfort. But I *had* to get Beth back. If that terrible voice was somehow connected to these kidnappings, I needed to find her *soon*. I looked up at Grey. "Let's get back to my place. I want to hear what you know."

Together, we hurried through the city. By the time we arrived at the street across from my flat, my skin was prickling with anticipation. The kidnappings and Grey's presence fought to dominate my thoughts. We might have broken the fated bond between us, but we hadn't broken the attraction.

I stepped off the pavement and into the street, my gaze on my flat. The motorbike came out of nowhere, going so fast that it seemed to appear from the blue.

Grey moved like lightning, gripping my shoulders

and spinning me around, putting himself between me and the bike.

It nearly hit him, missing by a margin of inches. My heart thundered as I panted, looking up to meet his gaze. Concern flickered in the depths.

"Are you all right?" he breathed.

"I don't know where my mind was." *On you.*

We stood so close that the heat of him radiated through me, his firelight and whiskey scent wrapping around me like a blanket. Protectiveness radiated from him.

He swallowed hard and stepped back, letting go of my arms. "Come."

He turned and looked both ways. The street was clear, so he crossed. I hurried after him, my gaze riveted to his broad back.

He'd put himself between me and danger always.

I knew it like I knew my own name. The bond between us was broken. It had taken with it some of the familiarity that I felt with him, some of the natural fit that we felt.

And yet, I still wanted him. We were more strangers than we'd ever been, but . . .

I still wanted him.

We reached the green door that led to the stairs up to my flat. As I unlocked it, Mac came careening around the nearby corner, her eyes brightening at the sight of us.

"You're back." Her short blonde hair was messy from the wind and her run. Her gaze flicked to Grey. "Did it work? Why is he here?"

"Third person, Mac." I raised my brows.

"Yeah, yeah. Apologies, Devil. But is the bond broken?"

"It is." His voice was stiff.

Relief flooded her gaze, then it landed on me. She frowned. "You look white as a ghost. What's wrong?"

"Beth was abducted." Just saying it made my stomach pitch.

"No." Mac whitened. "Really? From where?"

I repeated what Mary had told me.

"Shit." Mac frowned..

"Did you find anything?" I asked.

She shook her head, as though to clear it, then held out a little container of dirt. "Maybe, maybe not. This is a sample of the dirt from where the abduction took place, but I doubt it will tell you anything. I took it just because I felt weird leaving empty-handed."

I took the little container, knowing right away that it would be useless. Even a visit to the back garden where the girl had been abducted would be pointless—but I'd still probably go. "Thanks, Mac."

I opened the green door and took the stairs two at a time, Mac and Grey following. The door to my flat was slightly ajar, and I wasn't surprised to see a hint of

Cordelia's tail peeking out of the cupboard where I kept the snacks.

Normally, I'd tell her off. Her diet made me seriously concerned for the state of her arteries, but now wasn't the time.

I left her to it, hearing her crunch her way through a bag of her favorite pickled onion flavored corn snacks, and turned to Mac and Grey, who had followed me into my place. Quickly, I gave Mac an update about my power and the strange, terrifying voice that had called to me. How it had gone from violence to calm, angry to desperate.

"Whoa," Mac said. "That's weird."

"No kidding." I didn't want the attention, so I pointed to Grey. "Grey knows something about the abductions. So spill."

Mac turned wide eyes on Grey. "You do now, do you?"

"You know better than that, Mac. I'm not involved."

"Hmm."

"I've never dealt in people." His voice was hard.

Mac relented, nodding. "Fine, I do know that. You just make me wary because you're a risk to my friend here. I'm on edge."

"No longer," he said. "We've broken the bond."

Her gaze moved between the two of us, brows raised. The relief in her gaze had been replaced with curiosity. "Really?"

"Really." I nodded.

"Hmm."

"Quit with the 'hmms'." I turned to Grey, vowing to ask Mac more about her knowing noises. "Spill what you know. How do we find the kidnapper? And more importantly, how do we find *them*."

"It's not that easy." Grey leaned against the door jam and crossed his arms over his powerful chest. "Even if he's the one responsible, he has such a powerful and expansive underground network that finding the people he's taken is going to be nearly impossible. Deadly."

"I'm used to that. I just need a lead. Who is it?"

"Anton the Deceiver. A crime lord out of Monaco."

My heart thundered. A real lead, with a real location. I could so work with this.

"Yikes." Mac grimaced. "I've heard of him. Bad business, that fellow."

"Well, I'm going after him." I met Grey's eyes again. "Any tips?"

"I'm coming with you," he said.

"You can't. You heard what Cyrenthia said. We shouldn't be around each other. It's too dangerous."

"Why?" Mac demanded.

"We can't . . . fall for each other." I hesitated, feeling weird saying it in front of her. "Our bond as fated mates is broken, but fate is powerful. It could override the spell if we . . ."

When I trailed off, Grey interrupted, clearly not

liking the train of conversation. "You'll never make it into Anton's place alone. You can't just break in. And if you did, you'd be dead if you got caught."

"What do you mean?"

"Anton owns a casino in Monaco, in Monte Carlo. It's worth millions, and security rivals that on the Crown Jewels."

"*I* could." I crossed my arms over my chest.

He studied me for a moment, then nodded. "I do believe you could. Perhaps. But once you're in, you wouldn't be able to access him. It'd require more luck than exists in all the world, and if they catch you, there's no trial. There's no eviction. There's just execution."

The chill in his voice made me flinch, and I thought of the mob bosses we'd studied at the police academy. I'd seen what they were capable of, and they were the *human* ones. What could an evil, magical one do to me?

"I can get you in, and with a bit of luck, we can get an audience with Anton. Then you can ask your questions."

"But Cyrenthia..."

"I know the risks, Carrow. But the alternative is the lives of those who have been kidnapped. *Your* life if you get caught trying to break into Anton's place."

Shit. He was right.

There was so much at stake. *Beth*. The young girl. There was no time for me to be waffling about this. I needed his help, and I had the willpower not to fall for him. Especially now that our bond was broken. Half the work was done for me, for fate's sake.

"Okay, we do it your way," I said. "What does that entail?"

He thought for a moment, clearly running over the options in his mind. "Anton will be at his casino, though what he'll be doing is anyone's guess. He could be playing a game, watching a show, or torturing a minion."

"Sounds like a delightful guy," Mac said.

"He's unrepentantly terrible." Distaste curled Grey's lip. "I could set up a meeting, but it's unwise. It will put him on the alert, and he never wants to give a competitor what they want. If I had something to offer him, it would be different. But I don't."

"And we don't want to give a bastard like that anything," I said. "Especially not an inkling of what we want. He could hurt the victims if he knows we're after them."

"Precisely. So we need to be subtle. You and I will go to his casino as if we're out for a night on the town. Once there, we figure out what he is doing for the evening and find a way to join him."

"Then we kidnap him and question him?" I asked.

"Not quite, though it's an option. I'd like to avoid it due to the fact that he's bound to have dozens of guards and can lock the place down in a heartbeat. And my mind control powers will be blocked by the casino. The place is imbued with magic that makes him almost impervious."

I frowned. "How do we get him to talk, then? We can't bring him in for questioning legally. I've got no standing with any police." There actually were a few police in Guild City, though not as many as there would be out in the real world.

"And police can't touch him," Grey said.

"Truth serum, then," Mac said. "Or something that will make him susceptible to the Devil's mind control."

Grey nodded. "That's what I was thinking. We get close to him and try to dose him. I know a potion that will lower his defenses so that I can question him. The casino's protections shouldn't be a match against the combined magic."

I grimaced, thinking of how hard it would be to snag his drink and empty something into it.

"I can do it," Mac said.

I turned to her. "What?"

She shrugged. "I'm a bartender. You guys do your plan—get close to him. Get ready to ask your questions. I'll join the bar staff. It won't be hard to blend. When it's time, you signal me, and I bring him a spiked drink."

Grey gave her a considering look. "He's likely to have a specific server who deals with his drinks."

Mac shrugged. "I'll get clothes from the Fae shop that outfits spies. They'll definitely have something to help me blend. And for good measure, Eve can give me a potion to make me look like the server that I need to impersonate."

"That's possible?" I asked.

"Yes," Grey said. "Though those potions don't last long."

"Good thing I'm quick." She grinned. "And I know my way around a bar so well that no one will suspect me."

"It's too dangerous to break in," I said.

"I won't. I'll go to the server's entrance dressed as a server. People don't pay much attention to the staff."

Grey nodded. "I like this plan."

I didn't. It was too dangerous for Mac.

As if she could read my thoughts, she gave me a hard glare. "I've got this, Carrow. Beth was taken, remember? Not to mention the other girl. I'm going to help."

"Fine. Fine." I raised my hands in a placating gesture. "I know you do."

She nodded. "Damn right. And worse comes to worse, you carry a serum on you, just in case I need to bail."

I liked that safety-out. "Okay, it's a deal." I looked at Grey. "We can do this tonight?"

He nodded. "You're going to need clothes like the kind you wore to the speakeasy in Brasov."

I thought of the amazing magical dress that had made me punch harder and the stilettos that had felt like trainers. "I still have those."

"Their magic is dulled. You need new and better. Let me take care of it."

"Still taking care of me?" I hated to admit I liked it. "I thought we weren't bonded."

He opened his mouth, then closed it. Finally, he said, "I insist."

"Okay." I nodded, not wanting to fight.

"I'll meet you when you're done getting ready." He didn't wait for a response. Just turned on his heel and left.

Mac turned to me. "I don't know about this whole bond breaking thing, mate."

"What?" I frowned at her.

"There's still something between you."

I swallowed hard. "Yeah, well. I care for him."

"How much?"

"I honestly don't know."

Mac hovered her hand over my arm. "May I?"

"You want to read my future?"

"As much as I can." She gestured between me and the space where Grey had once stood. "Because I know you broke the mate bond, but things aren't over yet."

My heart began to thunder. If Mac had answers, I wanted them. I thrust my arm out toward her. She rested her fingertips on my bicep and closed her eyes. Her magic swelled, and I waited.

Finally, she opened her eyes. "I wasn't able to see much, but this thing between you . . . this breaking the bond . . .it doesn't mean it's over between you and Grey. Even this feels fated. Like it was meant to happen."

"Is fate really that powerful?"

"You have no idea." She shook her head. "You were trying to divert the course of fate by going to Cyrenthia and breaking the mate bond. But fate can't be tricked."

"Shit."

"Cyrenthia is right, though," Mac said. "If you want any chance at keeping the mate bond broken and saving Grey's life, you should try to stay away from each other."

~

Carrow

Hours later, after an amazing—though brief—visit to the Fae dress shop—Grey and I arrived in Monaco using a transportation charm. Monte Carlo, specifically. It was warm here, the scent of the Mediterranean wafting on an ocean breeze. The sound of waves crashing in the distance was audible over the low hum of traffic.

After getting kitted up in a generic bartender's uniform created by the Fae shop, Mac had taken a transport charm right to the casino, where she was currently sneaking in for her "shift."

Grey and I had appeared farther away since we needed to make a specific type of entrance. I turned to study the city. An infinite number of lights glittered all around, the gorgeous city lit up for the evening. Nestled on the coast between France and Italy, it was a dream destination for the likes of me.

Considering the fact that I was with Grey, it could have *been* a dream—broken bonds or not.

He looked like a million bucks, of course, wearing a tuxedo that had clearly been made especially for him. He was here to play a devilish game, all lethal strength and elegance, impossibly beautiful despite the cruel cast that had shadowed his face as soon as we arrived.

"You look different," I said. "Something about your face. Your expression."

His gaze flicked to mine, the coldness briefly replaced with warmth. "You can show nothing, here. Anton feeds on expressions like a shark."

I nodded, recognizing the same iciness he'd shown me when we'd first met. I'd thought he'd looked like the most beautiful statue I'd ever seen, so cold and hard and impenetrable that it made me want to crack him open even more.

"You look lovely," he said, his eyes warm.

Pleasure flushed through me, then I scowled. "No compliments. I'm a sucker for compliments, and I can't fall for you."

"Of course. You look like a hag."

I laughed, unable to help myself, and turned toward the street. My dress twirled around me, a glittery gold confection that made me feel like a princess. In addition to being gorgeous, it repelled blades and magic. It also enhanced my own powers, making my gift the slightest bit stronger, which I would need for what was to come.

The stilettos on my heels once again felt like trainers, and I knew I could sprint a mile in them. Hell, I could probably leap over a building in a single bound. The gem at my neck was actually a vial of truth serum, though no one would recognize it. Eve and the Fae dress shop owner had worked together to create it, though I might not have to use it. They'd done the same for Mac's uniform, and it would allow her to blend in with the rest of the staff.

As the sound of ocean waves crashed in the distance, Grey and I stood on a bustling city street, not far from Anton's club. An enormous Rolls Royce pulled up to the curb, gleaming brilliantly. It looked like something from the past, all elegance and beauty. The driver leapt out and opened the door for us, and I looked up at Grey. "For us?"

He nodded. "We need to blend in when we arrive."

He helped me into the car, his touch a brand. I barely resisted a shiver, and he withdrew his hands quickly.

"I'm sorry." His voice was low. "That was unwise."

Indeed, it was. Touching was about the dumbest thing we could do right now.

Inside the opulent car, I shifted over on the seat to

make room for him. He folded himself gracefully into the vehicle, and the driver took off, whisking us through the glittering streets of Monte Carlo.

"This is a lot different than the life I trained for," I mused, thinking of police college.

"Preferable, I hope?"

"Very." I stole a glance at him, then looked away, unable to bear his impossible beauty.

A few moments later, the sleek car pulled to a stop outside an enormous, ornate building. Golden lights lit up the marble facade, and a fountain shot sparkling water into the air. An aura of incredible wealth and danger gleamed around the place, and my heart raced, hope flaring.

With any luck, we were going to save the kidnapping victims tonight.

5

GREY

I climbed out of the car first, scanning the ornate court-yard for Anton's guards. Immediately, I spotted eight of them. I cataloged their weapons and species—what was visible, at least.

"Hey, let me out." Carrow's voice sounded from behind me, where I'd blocked her into the car on purpose.

Satisfied that it was safe, I turned and reached for her hand. She laid her palm in mine, and satisfaction surged through me.

No.

I couldn't feel those things anymore.

I *shouldn't*. The bond was broken.

My heart and body didn't seem to care, but I tried to shove the feeling aside anyway. I helped her stand, forcing my eyes off the way the glittering golden silk clung to her curves. Her eyes gleamed with interest as she looked around.

I turned, tucking her hand into the crook of my arm, and tried to see it through her eyes.

All around, people in glittering finery strolled up the stairs, looking beautiful and bored. It was an obscene amount of wealth on display, and distaste flickered through me.

"Is this not your scene?" Carrow asked.

"Hardly." I turned toward the massive entryway where Anton's goons guarded the doors.

They couldn't have looked more like a mob boss's henchmen if they tried. Big shoulders stuffed into tight suits, slicked back hair, and their magic on full display, the way humans would wear their guns visible.

I could feel their magic from where I stood, a billboard of a threat that was meant to keep the supernaturals in line. Not everyone in the crowd was magical, however, and the humans had no idea.

Sheep.

As if she read my thoughts, Carrow leaned close and whispered, "Are there humans here?"

"Yes. So no magical fights on the casino floor. Anton has a spell blocking most powers, especially around the gambling tables, but the goons are here to keep order as well."

"Ah, I see."

I caught the eye of one of the bouncers and raised two fingers in a clear signal. We wouldn't be entering through the normal way.

The man snapped to attention and turned, leading us to a side door.

"This way," I said. "We need to go through a different type of security."

"All of these wealthy people tolerate security?" she asked.

"To get in here, they do." I nodded toward the crowd we'd left behind. "Humans and low-power supernaturals go that way. More powerful supernaturals go this way."

"What is Anton looking for?"

"Any kind of threat. Magical weapons or particularly dangerous powers. If we tried to sneak through the human entrance, the sensors would catch us, and we'd be evicted."

She shivered. "You were right about this place being heavily guarded."

"We'll be fine. But we won't be able to use a transport charm until we are out of the building, so keep that in mind."

She nodded.

We neared the hulking guard, and he turned to open

an enormous golden door for us. I led Carrow into a spacious lobby. Crystal chandeliers gleamed overhead, shedding a sparkling light on the gold and velvet opulence of the interior.

It was Anton.

Like a petty king with too much money and no taste.

Two guards stood waiting for us, each at least seven feet tall. It was rare that I met someone taller than me, but it was immediately obvious that their size slowed them. Each wore a suit and held a slender black wand.

I leaned down to Carrow and whispered, "These men will check you for magical weapons, but they won't touch. Try to suppress your power as best you can."

She nodded, and I could feel her trying to draw it into herself. She'd become so much more proficient over the last few weeks, but her power had also grown. I could feel it inside her even now, expanding. Could she tell that it was doing that?

I had to assume so.

I did the same, making sure my magic was under lock and key. The men approached us, hovering their wands over our chests, then moving them around our bodies. I waited for the telltale vibration that indicated it had sensed something and was gratified when there was only silence. We didn't need to draw any attention to ourselves.

"They're clean," one of the guards murmured to the other.

One of the guards nodded. "You're done."

"Thank you." I took Carrow's hand again and tucked it into my arm.

We left the men behind, strolling into the main part of the casino. As we entered the enormous space, Carrow gasped. "Wow."

"I suppose it does make quite an impression." A lofty, vaulted ceiling was hung with even larger crystal chandeliers than the lobby. They were the size of cars, in fact. The gambling tables were gilt-edged, along with everything else in the godforsaken place.

"You really don't like it here, do you?" Carrow asked.

"No. It's an obscene use of wealth. And beyond that, in poor taste. Too much gold, too fussy, too ornate."

"Yes, I can see how you might not like that."

I looked down at her. "Know me so well, do you?"

She shrugged. "A bit."

I found I wanted her to know me better. I shouldn't want that now—our bond was broken. But I did.

A server in a small black cocktail dress approached, a tray of champagne glasses carefully balanced near her head. She smiled at us. "Drink?"

I took two. "Thank you."

She nodded and disappeared into the crowd. I handed one glass to Carrow. "Don't drink."

"No?"

I shook my head. "We need to see them made to be

sure they haven't been spiked with something. But we want to carry one, so we blend."

Even now, I could see two crime bosses that I recognized—one from the Chicago Dens and another from New York. Either would like to have me incapacitated and willing to spill my secrets.

"They aren't just meant to make us gamble more?" she asked.

"That's their purpose, yes. But they could be spiked. Either with something to lower our inhibitions or something worse."

She grimaced.

"Come." I drew her toward the bar. "We need a drink in hand so that people will lower their guards around us."

I was aware of her every movement as we walked toward the bar. The crowd parted easily to let us pass, and I stopped at an open spot at the long expanse of gleaming wood. At the far end, Mac appeared briefly, speaking to someone who looked like the manager. She blended perfectly, her hair darker and her face slightly different, thanks to Eve's potion. When she found her mark, she'd transform entirely to look like them.

Carrow and I both made a point not to look at her.

I leaned down and spoke at Carrow's ear, unable to help getting closer. It was unwise, but such a small thing could surely be forgiven by fate.

"What can I get you?" I asked.

"Sparkling water with a lime. In a rocks glass."

"Clever." It would look like a vodka soda or gin and tonic when served that way. I couldn't get away with anything less than an amber colored Scotch—Anton knew my preferences too well—but one drink would hardly affect me.

I withdrew a hundred-pound note from my pocket and made eye contact with the nearest server.

The small, pale man hurried over, a polite smile in his eyes. "May I help you?"

"I have a tab—Devil of Darkvale. My usual and a sparkling water with lime for the lady." I passed him the hundred-pound note, a not-so-subtle bribe that would encourage him to follow the notations on the valued client drinks list.

He took the note and nodded, hurrying off to the middle of the bar, where he retrieved a small black notebook.

Carrow nodded at him. "What's all that about?"

"They keep track of the preferences of the wealthiest visitors. I don't come here to gamble often, but I do come for meetings."

She raised her brows. "Crime lord meetings?"

I nodded. She winced, reminding me just how different our lives and values were.

Which was good. It would help us keep our distance when it was so vital that we do so.

I watched the bartender with a keen eye as he

cracked open a fresh bottle of my preferred Scotch. I didn't want anything that could be tampered with, and I was satisfied to see the small poof of blue magic that indicated a fresh, un-enchanted bottle. He poured a glass, then fetched a fresh bottle of Perrier and decanted it into a glass for Carrow.

When he'd returned with our drinks, we took them and turned to the room.

The space bustled with movement as people flowed between the tables, stopping to sit or stand at a game of chance.

"Any idea where Anton is?" Carrow asked.

I searched the floor, not spotting him in any of his preferred places. "He's either at a private table in the back or at the theater on the next floor."

A server strolled by, a tray of champagne raised high. I caught her gaze as she passed, and she stopped.

"Pardon me." I kept my voice low. "Where is Anton? I quite fancy a game."

She smiled widely. "Then it's your night. He's in the back. Good luck getting there."

I nodded. "Thank you."

She hurried on, and Carrow leaned up to speak close to my ear. "What does she mean about getting there?"

"It's a meritocracy at the back table. You need to earn your way there by winning out here."

"What game?"

"Poker."

Carrow grinned. "I'm good at poker."

"Are you now?"

"Very. Even without my gift."

"Then I'll stake you."

Her brows rose. "Really?"

"Really. I play, but not expertly. I've never had much interest. It will help our chances if both of us play."

"What if we lose?"

"Then we get clever and sneak in."

"I thought you said that was deadly."

"Exactly. So we should win."

She grimaced. "Well, we have a good plan, and I'm good at poker. Better when I can use my magic, but still good."

"That's where this comes in." I removed one of two small charms from my pocket and palmed it, then held her hand as if we were on a date. A streak of heat ran up my arm, and I couldn't imagine never touching her again.

Her hand tightened, closing around the sphere.

"Keep it out of sight," I murmured near her ear. "When you need to use your power, hold it to the underside of the table. It will adhere and break the spell that prevents you from using your magic."

She nodded. "Thanks."

"Come on, I'll get us chips and a seat at a table."

She tucked her hand into my arm, and we walked

across the casino. It was impossible not to feel the eyes of envious men—she was the most gorgeous woman in the room.

For tonight—and tonight only—she was mine. It might be just an illusion now that our bond was broken, but I didn't care.

6

CARROW

As Grey led me across the casino floor, the crowds parted to let us pass. I briefly allowed myself to imagine what it would be like if we were a couple.

A frisson of anxiety shot up my spine.

It was such a strange thought. Our bond was broken, and though I still felt something for him, without the bond to tie us together, it felt *crazy*. I'd known him such a short time, and he was *such* a bad idea.

He was a literal magical crime boss, the most feared man in Guild City and, also, the most dangerous. Everything about him should drive me away. A lot of things about him scared me, and without the bond to dull those feelings and draw me to him, I was able to actually feel that fright.

And yet, I still wanted him.

How could I not, when he acted and looked the way he did? Not only did he look like a fallen angel recently thawed from an icy sleep, he was always putting himself between me and danger.

I shook the thoughts away and focused on scouting out the casino. The exits were well-marked but also well-guarded. If there was a fire, we could all get out. Short of that, it looked like the bouncers would stop anyone from leaving without permission. They stood with their arms crossed and scowls on their faces, big bodies blocking the doors.

It didn't take long for Grey to arrange for chips and a spot at one of the top tables. The amount he'd requested made my head spin.

He handed me the chips and murmured, "My status might not get us an invite into Anton's meritocracy room, but we've got a seat at the next best thing. If we win enough at this table and, therefore, prove our skill, we'll be invited to Anton's private game next."

I took the stack of chips. "I've got this."

He smiled and nodded. "I believe it."

Grey and I joined the four other players at the table, and I carefully sized up my opponents. The skills I'd learned in interrogation training came in handy when playing poker. The many hours I'd spent playing with my colleagues were even more useful.

Everyone at the table—two women and two men—looked cool and collected. They were all dressed in exorbitantly expensive clothing, sipping champagne and whiskey while studying their cards. Though they had their signatures fairly well suppressed, I smelled magic on all of them. They could have been any species though—I still didn't have the skill to determine which.

The dealer was a stone-faced woman with smooth hands and a calming demeanor. She also wore her magic like a badge, and she was one tough cookie. I didn't know what she could do, but her power felt like a punch to the gut.

She leveled Grey and me with a serious gaze. "Five Card Stud. Twenty thousand dollar buy in."

The number nearly took my breath away, just as I'd gone a bit faint when Grey had requested half a million dollars in chips. It was an unimaginable amount of money.

But I kept my expression composed and pushed my chips toward the center of the table.

Grey did the same, and I was painfully aware of his every movement. It was almost like breaking our bond made me *more* aware of him, as if that were possible. It was the sense of the unknown, maybe, even though I *knew* I was supposed to avoid him.

The game moved quickly from there, and I got lucky

with the first few hands. Grey did too, or maybe he was just more skilled that he'd let on.

Either way, we advanced forward, hanging onto our spots at the table while one man and one woman dropped out. I drained my drink, and Grey ordered me another with a flick of his hand. It was a handy trick, since then he didn't have to let the rest of the table know I was only drinking water.

After two hours, during which I hadn't even needed to use the charm Grey had given me, we were the only ones left at the table. I was starting to get antsy, and the few glimpses I caught of Mac in her disguise just made me more nervous. If she were caught . . .

But hell, that went for all of us, and she was a big girl. She knew the risks. Didn't keep me from worrying about her, though.

"Sir? Madam?" A quiet, polite voice sounded from behind me, and I turned.

A slender gentleman with a pencil-thin mustache and an impeccable tux stood a few feet away, watching us expectantly.

"Yes?" Grey asked.

"His Excellency would like it if you joined him for a game, should you be willing."

His Excellency?

Okay, that was just too much.

Grey, ever the iceman, simply nodded. "I would enjoy that." He looked at me, a brow raised. "And you?"

I gave a brilliant smile. "Of course. Just let me powder my nose, and I'll be right there."

The man bowed, then gestured to the door that led to Anton. He disappeared, and Grey and I rose.

"I'll meet you over there." He nodded toward the door.

"All right." I hurried toward the bathroom, keeping a lookout for Mac.

She appeared right as I was walking down the hall toward the restroom. We didn't so much as pause, but I gave her a nod, indicating that it was time to swap places with the bartender who served Anton. She hurried off, and I made quick work of checking myself in the mirror. Everything was in place, and the gold dress still looked fantastic.

A few minutes later, I joined Grey. He looked amazing, standing alone near the door, his cold eyes surveying the casino. His tux fit his tall, broad build perfectly, and as he leaned against the wall, he looked like a predator lounging on the Savannah, waiting for some unwary prey to walk by.

When his eyes met mine, they warmed briefly. Then his face hardened, as if he'd noticed the softness. It was a bad idea in general, given our situation, but even worse while we were on Anton's turf. We'd agreed that my cover would be as Grey's new fling. If Anton sensed that he truly cared for me, he'd use me to hurt Grey. The last thing I wanted was to be a pawn in a battle between two mob bosses.

Grey held out his arm, and I took it. Together, we strode into the large room. It was beautifully decorated, though far too extravagantly, with a single table in the middle. Four players sat around it, Anton immediately recognizable.

It was just something about him—his aura, maybe, or the cold deliberation in his eyes. He made ugly, terrible decisions every day, and it was reflected on his face. So was the fact that those decisions didn't bother him a whit. Silver hair was swept back from patrician features, and his blue eyes were so pale they were almost colorless. His tux was as beautifully cut as Grey's, but his slender build didn't fill it out nearly as well.

Next to him sat an older woman with a tiny poodle in her lap. The poodle's poof of white hair matched her own, and the dress that she wore glittered pink under the crystal chandeliers. The last two figures at the table were vastly different—one man had black eyes and pale gray skin. He was utterly terrifying, actually, with a cold gleam in his gaze that was definitely snakelike.

The last man turned to look at us, a charming smile pulling up the corner of one side of his mouth. He was handsome, with a strong jaw and brilliant green eyes that complemented his dark hair. His tux fit him perfectly and, like Grey, he had the muscles to fill it out.

In fact, he looked like he should be out climbing mountains or crossing deserts in search of adventure.

"Welcome." Anton's voice was low and rich. "We could use some new blood in the game."

Grey and I strode to the table. He took the seat next to the scary man, and I sat between the poodle woman and the adventurer. She gave me a derisive look that was matched by her poodle—the little beast's lip even lifted in a growl. I turned my gaze away from the tiny monster and glanced at the man next to me.

He smiled charmingly. "It seems I got the lucky end of the seating arrangements. I'm Atticus Swift."

"Nice to meet you. Marie Stone." I gave him the fake name I'd worked up, not wanting Anton to remember me and seek me out.

Atticus held out his hand to shake, and though I'd normally avoid such a thing, I needed all the information I could get about my opponents. Knowledge was power, after all.

I gripped his strong hand and shook, suppressing a gasp at the images that flowed into my mind. Atticus, standing on the deck of a ship floating through the clouds, fighting off demons with a skill I couldn't help but admire. Another vision flashed—this time of him in an enormous, gorgeous office with a view of high rises in the distance. He had power and wealth, that was for certain. And a love of adventure.

Not only that—there was a distinct streak of honor

to him. He was some kind of thief; I was sure of it. But an honorable one. Unlike everyone else at this table—I didn't need to touch them to know they were shady as hell—he was a decent man. Albeit with a love of breaking the rules.

I tried to get an image of what his cards looked like —he had a hand in front of him—but the magic that surrounded the table made it impossible. It was an impressive spell, whatever it was, allowing my gift to work but not in a way that would allow me to cheat.

Damn.

At least I had the charm from Grey tucked into the top of my stockings, though it wouldn't be easy to deploy it with this crowd surrounding me.

The dealer, who I'd barely noticed until now, cleared his throat. The man was so bland looking—pale skin, pale hair, a soft face, and stooped shoulders—that he nearly blended with the background.

"Buy in is fifty thousand. One hundred to raise."

I tried not to let my jaw drop, but Atticus noticed my shock and leaned close. "Bit steep, I agree."

"Isn't that why you play here?"

He gave me a devastatingly handsome smile. Under any other circumstances, I might have flirted. I *should have* flirted. I should have done anything I could to tear my traitorous heart away from Grey. If it knew what was good for it, my heart would throw itself at Atticus.

As it was, I felt nothing when I looked at Atticus. He

might as well have been another species, albeit an objectively attractive one.

Unable to help myself, I glanced at Grey.

His eyes were slightly narrowed as he watched Atticus, and I could all but see the threat wafting around him.

Atticus leaned close to my ear and murmured, "I think your friend would like to knock my head against a wall."

Grey's eyes flashed, and he smiled coldly.

Oh, he could definitely hear Atticus, and he agreed.

I just smiled—hopefully in a mysterious way—and looked at the dealer expectantly. What I really wanted to do was jump on Anton and hold my knife to his throat, demanding answers.

But there were eight guards in the room, one at each corner and others at the door.

So, *that* approach was out.

The game began, moving swiftly at first. Anton was nearly silent, his gaze darting between the different players with the coldness of a snake's. When it landed on me, I had to suppress a shiver.

Surprisingly, the first person to leave the table was the terrifying man with the gray skin and black eyes. He hadn't said a single word the entire game—every signal he'd given to the dealer had either been a hiss or a tap on the table.

Finally, he lost spectacularly, and that was that.

Anton grinned with satisfaction when the man rose and slunk away toward the door, clearly pleased to have beaten him. So far, the mob boss was the best player at the table, though the rest were holding their own.

The woman in pink watched the cards avidly, her interest keen and her excitement high. Atticus, on the other hand, seemed bored. Almost as if he weren't here for poker at all and was just phoning it in with his bets. I shot him a glance out of the corner of my eye, and he grinned, almost as if he could read my curiosity.

Across the table, Grey looked between me and Atticus, his shoulders tense. Was he jealous?

We're not supposed to care about each other! I wanted to shout at him.

I merely looked away, catching the eye of the woman's little poodle. The creature glared at me, its eyes on my cards. I scowled back and tilted them in so the little cheat couldn't see them. Despite the fact that I could feel the magic-suppressing charm that surrounded the table, I wouldn't be surprised if he could telepathically convey to his owner what my hand looked like.

One hand in particular was so close, the betting so intense, that I nearly lost my spot at the table. Everyone else except for Atticus had folded, and the charming bastard was about to drive me away.

I could win this if I just had the slightest idea about his cards.

Now or never.

If I was going to use the charm that Grey had given me, this was the time. Carefully, I slipped my hand under the table and pulled the little charm out of the top of my stockings. Tension pulled my skin tight.

Please don't see me.

Grey coughed and nearly spilled his drink, and I wanted to shoot him a thankful glance. No question— he was trying to draw eyes away from me. Grey was so controlled and so smooth that he would *never* spill his drink.

Skin cold with nerves, I pressed the charm to the bottom of the table. Immediately, I could feel the suppression magic around myself deaden.

Casually, I pressed my knee against Atticus's under the table. Immediately, images flowed into my mind, bombarding me.

Atticus, bribing a guard. Then him sneaking around the back hallways of the casino, looking for something. *Interesting.*

I tried to direct my power toward his cards, wanting to get an idea of what he held. Or at least, whether he was bluffing.

Bluff.

The knowledge blasted into me. I couldn't see his cards, but the man was definitely bluffing.

"Well?" The dealer leaned toward me, his brows raised in question. "Fold or raise?"

I looked at Atticus, my lips pursed in thought. His gaze met mine, and the corner of his mouth quirked up in a smile. "Well?"

"Raise. One hundred and fifty thousand." My voice wanted to tremble when I said the words, but I suppressed it.

Atticus grinned knowingly and laid his cards face down on the table. "Fold."

I smiled and swept my winnings toward me, unable to believe that so much money was represented by little bits of plastic.

Next to me, the poodle growled low in its throat.

Shit.

I looked down at it, catching the menace in its eyes. The little bastard was onto me.

The old woman frowned at me, her pink lipstick matching her dress to perfection. She was about to accuse me—I could just feel it—when Cordelia appeared beneath the table.

I nearly jerked, surprised to spot the raccoon on the floor. My little sidekick reached up and grabbed the poodle's tail underneath the table.

Say anything, and I'll make you into my dinner. I do so love Poodle Fricassee. The threat in her voice was obvious, and the poodle stopped growling.

The woman, who hadn't noticed Cordelia, looked down when she realized that her dog had quieted.

"You're sure?" she asked the poodle.

The little dog glanced under the table at Cordelia, fear in its eyes. It nodded, and the older woman shot me a glare, then shrugged. "False alarm."

Cordelia disappeared, and the poodle relaxed. It still kept its gaze on me, but it didn't look like it was going to rat me out anytime soon.

"Madame Feriama's poodle is an excellent detector of cheats," Anton said smoothly.

My skin chilled, and I nearly fell out of my chair. Instead, I just barely managed to raise my eyebrows in a calm expression of interest. "You don't say?"

"Indeed." Anton watched me with interest.

"Next hand." Atticus grinned widely. "Let's not dawdle, I'm getting no younger."

I glanced at him, surprised. He clearly had my back, trying to get Anton's attention off me. His gaze flicked between the table and me.

He knows what I've done.

I smiled brilliantly, hoping it would throw him off. He huffed a small laugh, then turned toward the dealer as the cards were passed out.

The game continued uneventfully—or as uneventfully as it could when so much money was on the table. The woman and her poodle bowed out, and then it was just me, Grey, Anton, and Atticus.

Unfortunately, Atticus didn't seem like he was going to throw in the towel any time soon. The stakes just kept getting higher and the hour later, my concern for the kidnapping victims only growing.

Anton won another hand, then Atticus. Anton turned to one of the guards, his attention diverted from the table as he ordered another drink.

I glanced at the thief next to me, then gambled. I leaned close and murmured, "Don't you have some back hallways to sneak through?"

His brows rose slightly, and a tiny smile quirked the corner of his mouth. "Insightful, aren't you?"

"Yes. And I'll keep him occupied while you go and get about your business."

"You're not here for poker, are you?" His words were so soft and quiet against my ear that no one could hear them.

His posture, however, was another matter altogether. He was leaning close to me, his big shoulders curved inward like he was protecting me and his mouth close to my ear. It was a bullhorn that shouted *We're flirting.*

It was good cover and a smart move, despite the frown lines that cut deeply around Grey's mouth. Better for Anton to think we were flirting than conspiring against him.

And I wasn't supposed to be with Grey anyway.

"I'm not," I murmured back to Atticus. "And neither are you. So, go do your business while we do ours."

"Ours?" His gaze flicked to Grey, and he nodded. "I'll see what I can do."

Several hands later, after winning a sum of money that would buy me a nice flat in London, Atticus departed the table with a wave.

I caught Grey's eye.

It was time.

7

GREY

I watched Atticus rise and leave the table, something loosening inside me to see him putting distance between himself and Carrow.

I shouldn't care.

I knew I shouldn't. Not just because of the curse, but because she wasn't *mine*. No matter how much my soul screamed it, she wasn't.

My gaze lingered briefly on Carrow, unable to resist her beauty. She pressed her fingertips to the golden charm at her throat, contacting Mac.

It was time.

"Well, it's just the three of us now, isn't it?" Anton's eyes glittered with the thrill of the hunt.

I'd never enjoyed poker—too often it sat you next to the likes of Anton. I didn't let it show on my face, however, and gave the bastard my best bland smile.

"Are you sure you aren't here for other reasons, Devil?" Anton asked.

Of course I was.

I rarely joined him at his table, and only when I wanted something. My gaze flicked to Carrow. "My lovely companion enjoys the game."

"She is quite talented." The gleam in his eyes made me want to tear his head off and feed it to the old woman's poodle.

I tightened my grip on my cards, pulling myself back at the last moment to keep from crushing them.

"And I'm going to beat you." Carrow smiled mysteriously. "You won't even see it coming."

Anton leaned forward. "I quite like you.'

And I'd quite like to smash your face in. I looked at the dealer. "Next hand, please."

As much as I didn't enjoy poker, I'd rather play it than watch Anton leer at Carrow. The man turned his attention back to me as he idly took his cards. "What is your true purpose for being here?"

I thought quickly, needing a reason. He'd never believe that I was just indulging Carrow's whims for poker. "I'm looking into starting an export business. Magical arms."

I didn't generally deal in weapons—or at least I was

extremely cautious who I sold to—but Anton had his fingers deep in that pie. It was a particular interest of his, arming petty warlords in developing magical communities.

"Oh?" Anton's brows rose.

"Yes. I thought we might find a mutually beneficial arrangement."

"Why not discuss it at a meeting with me?"

I gestured to the table. "I know how you enjoy this."

"Wanted to put me in a good mood, did you?"

"You could say that. And I wasn't willing to wait to speak with you."

"Ah, yes." He steepled his fingers in front of his face. "I am rather hard to get ahold of."

He made people wait for the hell of it, as a way to establish dominance. It was a petty trick that didn't work on me.

At the edge of the room, a server entered, a tray balanced on her shoulder.

Mac, thank fates. She looked different, with long red hair and a round face. The potion she'd taken had worked wonders to change her into Anton's usual server, though I could see the hint of green eyes that looked like her.

Carrow carefully kept her gaze on her cards as Mac approached and leaned down to serve Anton his drink. He leered at her and smacked her on the arse. I clenched my fist, barely resisting the urge to beat him. Ire flashed in Mac's eyes, and her hand twitched.

We both ignored him, and she disappeared out of the room. Anton took a sip immediately, then another. His eyes went slightly hazy, and I felt it when the spell that protected him broke. Almost as if a window into his mind had been opened, and now I could see inside.

Carrow's gaze scanned the room and, swiftly, I did the same, taking in the guards who stood at the edges. They were far enough away that they couldn't hear, and as long as Anton didn't signal them, we were in good shape.

"Anton, care to tell me what your hand is?" I smiled at him.

"An ace and a two." Truth rang in his voice.

"Excellent." I laid my cards on the table, no longer interested. "Where are the kidnapping victims?"

Real confusion flickered in his eyes. "Kidnapping victims?"

"The ones that your men have taken. Red eyes that flicker like flame. You're the only one who uses minions like that."

"Ah." Understanding dawned in his eyes. "*That* job." He shrugged. "I do not know."

"Yes, you do," Carrow snapped.

Anton's gaze moved to her, irritation flickering in his eyes, the faint fog disappearing from the irises.

"Anton, look here." I imbued my voice with my magic, drawing his attention to me.

He turned back, his eyes foggy once more. I shot Carrow a quick look and shook my head. It needed to be my voice asking the questions, otherwise he might fall out from under my spell. She scowled but nodded.

I turned to Anton. "You're saying that someone hired you to kidnap those people?"

Anton nodded. "Indeed."

"Who?"

He shrugged, bored. "No idea."

"You don't care where the money came from?"

"Of course not. It all spends the same."

He was right about that, and I often felt the same. Unfortunately, it didn't help me at all here. I focused on the biggest questions. "Are the victims alive?"

Disinterest gleamed in Anton's eyes, along with confusion. He was fighting the pull of my voice, though ineffectively. He shrugged. "The orders were to bring them alive and unharmed, so I assume so."

"Where to?"

"That, I also do not know. My men are given transport charms with a specific end destination that they do not know. Once they have the target and deliver them using the charm, their memory is wiped. None of the four can remember a thing."

Carrow's foot nudged mine under the table, and I looked at her in time to see her mouth the word *four?*

I turned to Anton. "You've abducted four? All from Guild City?"

"Yes. All in the last three days."

Why hadn't Carrow or I heard about the first two? Perhaps they had no friends or contacts, but still...

"You truly know nothing about the one who has ordered these jobs? How do you communicate?" I asked.

"Through the network, of course."

Damn. I'd been worried about that. The network was a magical system of communications between members of the criminal underworld. It was comprised primarily of mercenaries and kingpins who would do any job for hire, and anonymity was guaranteed. Most people didn't want to be known for their criminal activity, and the network made it possible for politicians and other upstanding citizens to hire the services of those who worked outside of the law.

Essentially, anyone could be behind this.

"The messages appeared on my desk, as you well know," Anton said. "No signature, just a job and the down payment, along with the transport charms for my men."

"How do you choose who to kidnap?" I asked.

"The request is always for a supernatural with a particular talent, but it doesn't matter *who* exactly."

"But why from Guild City?"

Anton shrugged. "It's convenient for me. Full of all kinds of Magica, and I have a contact there who finds me what I need. I tell him what magical talent the client requires—he finds the person and gives me a name. Then my man retrieves the target."

"Like a talent scout for evil," Carrow muttered.

It was so neat and tidy. "Who is your contact in Guild City?"

"A mage in Hellebore Alley. Christoph Venderklein."

I wasn't familiar with the name, but I would find him. "What types of supernaturals have you acquired so far?"

"A lion shifter, a fire mage, a seer, and a witch, but the client never said why they wanted those talents."

There had to be a pattern there. "Do you have any more of those transport charms?"

"No, I gave the last one to my man just a few hours ago."

Across the table, Carrow stiffened.

"Does that mean another job is going to take place?"

"At least one more, yes."

"When?"

He glanced at the large, ornate clock hung high on the wall. "Around now, in fact."

"Where?" I demanded.

"Why, outside of the Witches' Guild in your fair city. The client wanted another powerful witch."

Another?

I could feel Carrow vibrating to demand answers, to dart away from the table. Fear and worry radiated off her like an aura. She was friends with the witches, I recalled, and Beth's abduction had hit her hard. "Any witch in particular?"

"No, just one with a skill for spells."

"Thank you for the game, we need to go." Carrow stood, swept her chips into her little handbag, then turned and strode toward the doors. The guards darted off the walls, moving to intercept her.

I met Anton's gaze. "Forget these questions immediately."

He nodded, and I lunged upright, sweeping my chips off the table, and moving toward her. The guards were nearly to Carrow now, clearly having been ordered to stop anyone who left too abruptly. A quick, unexpected exit from a card game was always suspicious.

I felt my hold on Anton snap, and glanced back. He looked at the table, then at us.

Shit.

We'd left too abruptly, right in the middle of a hand, with a good bit of our money still in the middle of the table. No one in their right mind would do that. Confusion flickered in his eyes.

He didn't remember me tampering with his mind, but he knew something was up. This was all too strange to be normal. He waved a hand at the guards, his voice cracking like a whip. "Stop them."

The guards lunged for Carrow, and she swung out at the first, delivering a devastating punch to his face. The blow was assisted by her magical dress, and his head snapped back, and blood flew from his mouth. He landed hard on the ground, skidding backward.

A second guard attempted to punch her in the stomach, but his fist bounced off the silk of the dress and he shrieked, the bones in his hand shattering. Carrow kicked him in the gut with her stilettos and whirled on another guard. She had always been a good fighter, but the dress made her phenomenal.

I drew two daggers from the ether and hurled them at the guards nearest her. The blades found their marks in the chests of the men, who slammed to the ground like redwoods.

Anton's chair scraped as he rose, but I paid him no mind. He was powerful because of his cunning, not because of his brawn or magic, and Carrow needed me.

I sprinted to her, dragging one of the guards away and snapping his neck. Killing him went too far—in the back of my head, I knew it—but I couldn't stop myself. She was threatened, and all I could see was red.

Apparently, it didn't matter if we shared the mate bond. I'd be driven to protect her no matter what.

The fight was over in seconds, the guards landing on the ground like refuse when we were done with them. I spun around, spotting Anton speaking into his comms charm.

Well, shit.

I couldn't kill him, though. It would put a target on

my back. Worse, it would put a target on Carrow's. It was one thing to wreak havoc on a rival's turf . . . it was entirely another to kill the rival. The network didn't stand for that.

"Come on." I grabbed her hand and we ran for it. We just had to make it to the outside of the building. If we could get onto the main gaming floor, which was only ten meters away, Anton's guards would be less likely to use magic against us. They wouldn't want to scare the humans who were spilling their money into Anton's pockets.

Carrow and I raced out into the main part of the casino, joining the throng that milled around the tables. Guards moved away from the walls, converging on us.

I caught sight of Mac behind the bar at the same time Carrow did. Her face had returned to normal, and she gestured for us to head her way.

"Come on." Carrow pulled me toward her, and we darted between the tables.

As we ran, Carrow yanked a cell phone from her bag and frantically dialed a number. She raised the phone to her ear and spoke quickly. "Eve, the kidnappers are going for someone else at the Witches' Guild. You have to tell them."

A guard neared us, and I let go of Carrow's hand, putting myself between her and the bastard. His brow twisted with anger as he raised a fist, but I was faster, punching him hard in the face. He reeled backward, collapsing on a spinning Roulette table. The people standing around the thing shouted and jeered, but we kept moving.

Two more guards tried to intercept us, but we laid them out with punches.

Finally, we reached the bar.

"This way!" Mac led us through a door into a service hallway that was far more austere than the casino itself. "There's an exit this way."

She raced down the hall, and we sprinted after her. Guards spilled into the hall behind us, and Carrow turned around, taking off her Fae silver bracelet and hurling it at them. The jewelry clattered to the ground in front of them, exploding in a blast of silver smoke that slammed into my back.

I nearly stumbled, but the guards were thrown backward. Smoke filled the hall behind us, temporarily covering our retreat.

We reached the door a moment later, and Mac threw herself against it, pressing on the bar to open it.

The thing stayed shut.

"Shit!" She pushed harder. "It was open when I came."

Damn it. "They've locked the place down." I turned, searching the hall that stretched down to our left.

A figure appeared, tall and familiar.

That bastard Atticus. I recognized him from my network contacts. He advertised his work as a form of security. I knew who to go to if I ever wanted something 'liberated' from a vault.

His gaze moved to Carrow. "You really weren't here for the poker."

"No, do you know a way out of here?"

He raised a brow. "I do, but you've interrupted my job with this little alarm situation."

His job? Clearly the bastard was up to something.

"A thousand apologies," Carrow said. "We're trying to save some people's lives, so you're going to need to get over it and help us."

Atticus gave a wry grin. "This way."

I didn't want to trust the bastard, but Carrow grabbed my arm and yanked me forward. We sprinted after him, following him into an even smaller service hall and an empty office. A window was propped open with a magical charm that glowed bright green.

"Quick," Atticus said. "The charm is about to give out. The casino's security is weakening it."

"Thank you." Carrow hurried to the window and scrambled out.

Mac gave Atticus a quick up and down as she passed. "I'm Macbeth O'Connell. You're ever in London, stop by the Haunted Hound."

Atticus smiled. "I just might."

She nodded, then climbed out the window.

I met Atticus's gaze as I passed. "Thank you. Are you following?"

He shook his head. "This is perfect for me. They'll be so busy trying to find you that they won't notice me slipping into the back."

I didn't know what was in the back, and I certainly wasn't going to ask. "Best of luck."

He nodded, then disappeared back into the building. I followed Mac and Carrow out into the breezy Monaco night.

Carrow dug into her pocket and withdrew a transport charm. She hurled it to the ground. A poof of silvery dust exploded upward, and she reached for our hands. Mac and I grabbed hold of her.

As we stepped into the transport charm, I prayed we weren't too late.

8

CARROW

The ether spun me through space. My stomach heaved, a byproduct of the ride and the nerves that raced through me.

Please let us be in time.

I couldn't bear for there to be another abduction. And not another one of the hilarious, spunky witches who were my new friends.

The ether spit us out into the cool night air at the edge of the Witches' Guild square. It was the closest I could get, and the abandoned, weed-filled space separated us from the crazy Witches' Guild tower. The abandoned shops were silent at our back, and the moon rose high behind the tower where the witches lived.

The square structure was built of wood and beige plaster, with dark oak staircases winding around the exterior. It leaned slightly to the left, with a pointed roof that looked like a witch's hat. Green smoke belched from the many chimneys. Magic sparked all around, but my gaze was drawn to the great blue bonfire rising from an old stone well at the side of the property.

A woman danced around it, her pale limbs gleaming in the moonlight. Dark feathers decorated her body, and midnight smoke snaked around her ankles. She chanted something that I couldn't hear.

"It's Coraline," Mac said. She began to scream Coraline's name, but the witch clearly didn't hear her. She just kept dancing and chanting, in some kind of trance. "Why the hell is she outside alone with kidnappings going on?"

"The witches had no reason to think they'd be targeted twice."

From behind, I heard Eve's voice. She was shouting frantically, and I turned, spotting my Fae friend flying low to the ground, yelling into a cell phone.

She was still trying to contact the witches. Her raven flew behind her, eyes on me.

A connection sizzled between me and the bird. I spun back to Coraline and sprinted toward her, Grey and Mac at my side. From behind, I could hear a voice shriek out of the cell phone that Eve still held.

The witches knew.

At that moment, the main door burst open and four witches spilled out onto the landing. Mary, along with two that I didn't recognize. They sprinted down the rickety, winding staircase that led to the ground.

Just as they reached it, a man appeared right out of thin air, only fifteen feet from Coraline.

We were still eighty feet away, and the witches weren't much closer.

Coraline, still in the grip of a magical trance that had turned her eyes into inky pools of midnight that I could see even from this distance, didn't even notice him. He grabbed her from behind, and she shrieked.

The bonfire died immediately, as if her magic had been severed.

"Electo liquernum," Mary shouted, her voice carrying over the sound of Coraline's scream. She waved her hand, and sparkling water surged up from the well. It slammed into the kidnapper, nearly driving him away from Coraline.

She stumbled backward, breaking his grip on her arm, but he flung out his hand and the water splashed back into the well. He reached for Coraline, but Eve's lightning slammed into him.

He barely even flinched, instead reaching out and grabbing Coraline before she could run away. He yanked her to him, pulling her against his chest as he reached for his pocket.

No.

We couldn't let him get to his second transport charm.

Beside me, silver flashed as Mac hurled a dagger at him. The blade struck him in the arm that reached for his pocket, and he howled, spinning backward.

We were almost to him. Only thirty feet away. Grey, with his incredible speed, was even closer.

The kidnapper didn't even bother to remove the steel that lodged in his flesh. Instead, he raised his impaled arm and waved it, dark magic flashing on the air. It smelled of sewage and crawled across my skin like spiders.

Thousands of knives appeared in the air, floating between us and him. The blades pointed toward us, glinting evilly in the moonlight.

One of the witches shrieked her rage. They were nearly to their sister, but the blades stood in their way. The witch on the far left—one that I didn't recognize—waved her hand and conjured a tornado. The other witches raised their hands and directed their magic toward the whirling wind, helping their coven member.

The tornado tore through the blades, sucking them up and pulling them away.

Grey was nearly there. He made his move, sprinting toward the kidnapper, who was once again reaching for his pocket. He grabbed the man by the arm and tore him away from Coraline, who stumbled forward. She appeared dazed, as if the kidnapper's touch had addled her mind and magic.

I reached her, grabbing her to pull her farther away.

The kidnapper roared, a massive burst of magic exploding out from him. Grey was blasted backward, thrown fifteen feet across the lawn. The blast slammed into me as well, nearly pulverizing my insides.

I almost went to my knees, but managed to keep my grip on Coraline, who almost seemed sedated by the villain's touch.

The bastard surged for us, and I shoved him back hard.

The contact blasted through me, sending an image into my mind, burning it behind my eyes.

A twisted serpent design, ornate and unfamiliar.

Crimson red filled my vision, along with the screams and shouts of war. The smell of blood. The taste of dirt.

The kidnapper reached for us again, slamming a hand into me that felt like touching a live wire. Electric shock blasted me backward, my vision temporarily blind. Panic flared as I lost my grip on Coraline and flew through the air, slamming into the ground.

One quick shriek sounded, and I scrambled upright, my vision still bleary. Through hazy eyes, I caught sight of Coraline disappearing into a cloud of orange smoke, her witch sisters only inches away from grabbing her.

Shit.

The orange cloud disappeared entirely, and I ran for

it, desperate to get a hint of where the bastard had taken my friend.

I plowed through the line of confused witches, stumbling to a halt in the space where the cloud had just been. I used all of my magic to try to get an idea of where they'd gone, but nothing came.

It was as if they'd never been there at all.

My heart thundered in my ears, and adrenaline weakened my knees.

"We're too late." My words escaped on a whisper.

"What the hell just happened?" Mary demanded, her pink hair flowing in waves down her back. Ire flashed in her magenta eyes. "Did you know there would be a second abduction?"

"No." Horror turned my stomach. "Not until just five minutes ago." Damn, this guilt burned. We should have been quicker at the casino. If only I'd won my hands a little faster. If only we'd avoided the bar all together.

Mary waved her hands. "More details, Sherlock. Because we've been trying to find Beth and have had no luck."

"We haven't figured out where she is yet," I said.

"Well, figure it out faster," Mary snapped.

"Rudeness is not necessary." Grey stepped between me and the witches, his posture protective. "Carrow is doing everything she can to help your friend and the other victims. You should be thanking her, not criticizing."

I pressed a hand to his back. "It's all right."

"It's not." His voice was firm and restrained, as if he were holding himself back for my sake.

The witches glowered at him, but they nodded.

"Come." Mary waved a hand for us to follow her into the Witches' Guild tower. "Let's go inside and discuss this. I want to know what you've found."

"Of course." I nodded.

"Are they going to kill her?" Mary asked. "Have you learned that, at least?"

"I don't think so. Not yet. Not soon." God, it was all so confusing. "Not until they've accomplished their goal, at least."

"Which is?" Mary asked.

"Inside," Grey reminded.

"Yeah, yeah." Mary hurried toward the tower, racing up the rickety steps toward the main door.

We followed, and I shot Grey a grateful look. He was carefully looking ahead, not making eye contact with me, which was for the best.

Jeeves, the staid butler, waited for us at the door. His expression was bland, and his lips pursed as we walked by him. Normally, he might make a snide comment to Mac about not thieving, but he was able to read the room and kept his mouth shut this time.

Mary led us down the narrow, dark hallway toward a room I'd never entered. The entire place was a jungle. As soon as I stepped in, the air grew more humid.

Crickets sang through the dim space, their chorus nearly deafening.

In front of me, Mary's shoulders seemed to relax.

The plant-filled room was clearly her happy place, though I had a hard time understanding why.

The plants that covered the walls all had *fangs*. They were like crazy magical versions of Venus Fly Traps, or something out of that old movie, the *Little Shop of Horrors*.

Two massive couches filled the space, facing each other but separated by a dark, gleaming pool of water. A glass table sat over the pool, giving a clear view of the frogs that sat on the huge lily pads.

In the corner, an enormous alligator yawned.

Mary threw herself onto the couch, gripping the bridge of her nose with one hand. "We've had no luck tracking Beth. Tell me you've found something."

The other witches joined her on the same couch, and my group took the one that faced them. Grey stayed standing, leaving room for Mac, Eve, and myself. There was technically room for him, but I could tell he was trying to maintain his distance.

It was the only smart thing, even though I wanted to be near him. It was a terrible idea, and our bond was broken, yet the desire was strong.

I leaned forward. "We've learned that the kidnappers have taken people with specific magical skills. So they must want them for something, and until that thing is done, they must be alive."

"Them?" Mary asked. "How many?"

I leaned toward the witches. "There have been four kidnappings in Guild City recently. Five, with Coraline."

"What?" Shock flashed in Mary's eyes. "That's more than we thought."

As I told them everything we'd learned from Anton, more witches piled into the room. They perched on windowsills and leaned against the walls as the flesh-eating plants stroked their hair. Over a dozen of them sat around the pond, their eyes riveted on me.

"Anton the Deceiver?" Mary nearly spit on the name. "That bastard."

"He's not the one behind it all," I said. "But we don't know who is."

"Whoever it is, he's going after supernaturals with particular gifts, right?" Mary asked.

"And there's a symbol connected to him," I said, only now remembering the image that had blasted into my head when I'd shoved the kidnapper. "Could I have pen and paper, please?"

"Sure." Mary waved a hand. As if he'd been hovering nearby with the supplies at the ready, Jeeves appeared.

He handed me parchment and an old pen, and I leaned down and sketched out the design on the paper. My hand shook as I remembered the flashing red that had flared in my mind. It had been the exact shade of blood, and the sounds had been those of war.

I'd seen the same thing in the alley where Beth had been abducted. It had to do with the kidnappings— somehow linking me to them—but I had no idea how.

I forced my mind back on the symbol I'd seen. It came easily from memory, the lines flowing from my mind to my hand. Soon, the scrolled image was sketched out, the snakes twisting around each other in a complicated knot.

I held it up and showed the witches. "Does anyone recognize this?"

Everyone shook their head, and I frowned, looking between Mac, Eve, and Grey. None of them said anything, and I turned back to Mary.

"You should go to Seraphia's library. She might have something for you," she said. "In the meantime, we're going to work on tracking charms. No way in hell we're letting that bastard keep Beth and Coraline."

"We'll get them back," I promised.

"Keep us updated," Mary said. "We'll work on this from our end, and you go at it from yours. Any leads and we let each other know."

I nodded and stood. My friends joined me, and we left the witches' creepy room, dodging the women crowding the floor. Half of them glared at us, as if we'd been the ones to abduct Beth and Coraline. I ignored them. It wasn't that different than Police College, honestly.

The night was cool and dark as we stepped out onto the rickety stairs that led to the ground. Moonlight illuminated the weedy yard and the well where Coraline had been dancing.

"It all happened so fast," I murmured.

"Anton has powerful employees," Grey said. "Though *that* was unusual. Whoever is hiring him is paying a pretty penny to get that kind of service."

"I've never seen anything like it," Eve said as she typed into her phone. She caught sight of my questioning glance. "Calling Seraphia and seeing if she can let us into the library right now."

The phone rang, the tinny sound echoing across the night as we descended the rickety stairs. It went straight to voice mail—the pre-recorded option, not a personalized one by Seraphia.

Eve tried four more times on the way home, but the librarian never picked up.

"That's strange," Eve said. "Seraphia and I have been hanging out quite a bit lately, and she always picks up."

"Even at this hour?" I asked, noticing that the Devil was walking alongside us, his phone pressed to his ear.

Eve nodded. "I called once about this infomercial I thought she'd like. It was hilarious. She picked up at 2am."

"Do you think she's okay?" Worry echoed in Mac's voice. "She hasn't been abducted, has she?"

I nodded. "Doubtful. Anton would have told us if there was a job out for her."

"Unless it was just hired," Eve said.

"It's only been thirty minutes since we saw him last. He couldn't coordinate that quickly, not when his contact in Guild City needs to find him a suitable target," the Devil said.

"We'll try tomorrow morning. We need sleep anyway. Just a bit." Surprise flickered through me when I realized that we had already reached my street. I looked at Grey. "Your place is that way."

He nodded. "Just wanted to make sure there was no trouble on the way back."

"Thanks." I studiously kept my gaze on my green door instead of on him. The savory scent of kebabs wafted from the shop next door, and my stomach grumbled.

As if he'd read my mind, Berat stepped out of the shop, a pile of takeout containers in his hands. He raised them and smiled at us.

I stopped in front of him. "What's all this? We didn't place an order."

Berat nodded at Grey. "The Devil did."

"You sure eat a lot," Mac said.

The smallest smile quirked the corner of Grey's mouth. "It's for you. It's been a long day."

Holy crap, he had gotten me food.

"There's one for Cordelia as well," he said.

As soon as her name was called, the raccoon appeared, her masked gaze riveted to the stack of glass takeout containers. A toothy grin stretched across her face.

"You can't do things like that," I blurted.

His gaze flicked to mine. So did everyone else's.

Heat flooded my cheeks. "I mean, we're supposed to maintain our distance." *And doing thoughtful things like making sure I have dinner is a surefire way to get me to fall even harder for you.*

I didn't say the last bit, though.

"Of course." His voice was slightly stiff, but there was a knowing gleam in his dark eyes. He stepped backward, clearly about to head home. "I am going to set spies on Anton's casino. And I'll search for his contact here—the one who finds the kidnapping victims. I will alert you if I learn anything new."

"Thank you."

He turned and walked away, his huge form graceful as he strode down the street. The moonlight gleamed around him, making him appear otherworldly. Something pinched in my chest as I watched him walk away, and I turned to Berat.

He handed over the containers, and I took them. "Thank you."

He nodded, his eyes dark with confusion, then

disappeared back into the restaurant, which appeared to be closed. Of course it was closed at this late hour, but nothing was *really* closed if Grey wanted something.

Silently, our group walked up the stairs to my flat. Normally, Cordelia would be literally jumping with joy at the sight of the kebabs, all but climbing my legs.

Even she was silent.

I walked into my flat and handed out the food.

Mac took it but didn't open it. Instead, she just stared at me. "I don't think your bond is really broken."

I sighed. "It is. I can feel it. I swear to God, it was like a wire snapped. It *is* broken."

"But there's still something between you," she said.

"I care for him. Like, really care for him. It's emotions, not some magical bond."

"And he cares for you," Eve said.

"Yeah." The word rushed out of me, and I collapsed on the couch. "I think we were maybe a bit too late in breaking the bond."

"You'll just have to stay away from each other," Mac said.

"You're right." I leaned my head back on the couch. "I'm not in love with him or anything. It's just that I *like* him. And I can't help it."

"Well, try," Mac said. "Because your lives depend on it."

That night, I dreamed. Maybe it was the kebabs that I'd scarfed down, or maybe it was the fact that I'd seen Grey right before bed.

But I couldn't help it.

He appeared in my dreams, tall and strong, and so very *present*.

So present that it almost didn't feel like a dream at all. I was in my bed, just like in the real world. It was his presence I felt first, powerful and comforting. I opened my eyes, spotting him on the other side of the room, standing in the doorway.

His posture was hesitant, his expression unsure.

I sat upright, dragging the quilt over my ratty old T-shirt. It was one of Beatrix's that I'd never let go of, but it was in such bad shape I only wore it to bed.

The moonlight cut through the windows, gleaming pale white on his face and bare chest. He wore only a pair of sleep pants, a dark silky material that hung low on his hips, giving the most perfect view of the muscles that arrowed downward. Despite his massive size and ridiculously sculpted body, the light almost made him appear angelic, which was insane for a man rightfully called *The Devil*.

"Are you really here?" I asked.

"I'm not sure." He raised his hand, inspecting it curiously. "I was just in my bed."

Had I really conjured him? Or was this just the best dream ever?

He looked so amazing standing in the moonlight that I wanted to believe I was dreaming. *Of course* I was dreaming. It was insane to think otherwise. I didn't have that kind of power.

And all I wanted in the world was him.

I beckoned to him, determined to enjoy the dream for all it was worth. It would be gone in the morning, and all I would have was memories. Memories of an act that had never happened—not truly, at least—but that didn't mean I couldn't enjoy it. Anyway, Dream Me didn't need to be totally rational and wise.

9

GREY

Carrow gestured to me from her bed. The scene had the vaguely filmy quality of a dream. Almost as if the edges were blurred and reality distorted.

I'd never dreamed much—not since being turned, at least. The only visions that visited me in the night were horrible memories of atrocities I'd committed while under the influence of the blood lust.

Never had an apparition like Carrow appeared in my mind.

But now that she had, I ached to walk toward her. She was so beautiful in the bed, her golden hair tousled and the moonlight gleaming in her eyes. Her lips were impossibly soft-looking, and the memory of our one night together flashed through me, making heat coil tight.

I wanted that again.

I would *always* want that.

And even if this dream was a terrible idea, it was just a dream. And I wanted it. She wanted it.

I strode toward her, desire spiking through me, coiling low in my groin and causing me to go unbearably hard. Memories of her taste lingered on my tongue, and if I could only have it again in dreams, then I would take it.

I reached her, towering over her.

Something dark and terrible in me delighted in the difference in our size. She was strong. Powerful. But she was also so much smaller than me. So much finer and more beautiful.

It was such a contrast to the darkness of my life, the harshness.

I yanked the covers away from her, and she gasped. Moonlight fell on her long legs and the white cotton between her thighs. My mouth watered, and my fangs threatened to descend. I wanted to taste her there. To bite, right on the soft flesh of her thighs. To hold her hips and keep her still as I ate my fill.

I clenched my fists, resisting the urge, and put a knee on the bed, looming over her and thanking a God I didn't believe in for a dream I'd never forget.

"Grey." Her voice was husky as she reached up to grip my shoulders.

Her hands clutched at me, and I leaned into her touch, reaching down to grip her hips. She looked so delicate in my big hands, the torn T-shirt riding up her midsection to reveal the soft curve of her stomach.

"Carrow." Her name escaped on a growl, and hunger rose in me.

She spread her thighs, and I caught sight of the shadow there.

Just one more taste.

I dragged her down the bed, too rough for real life but perfect for the dream. Carrow gasped, her gaze flicking to mine as she lay flat on the bed.

I gave in to my baser urges. It was a dream, after all.

In one harsh motion, I tore the tiny scrap of cotton away from her hips, revealing her to the moonlight and to me. She arched toward me, so perfect and beautiful.

I fell between her thighs, burying my head between them as I gripped her hips tight, unwilling to let her get away.

Instead of struggling, she wrapped her thighs around my head until my entire world was consumed by her. Her scent, her taste, her wetness.

Her cries echoed in the room as I tasted her deeply, devouring her like it was the last time.

Please don't be the last time.

If all I could have were dreams like this, I would take

them. If there was only this one dream, this one last scrap of her resurrected by my memory and fantasies, I would take it and remember it forever.

It didn't take long to drive her over the edge, almost nothing at all to make her scream and squirm in my arms.

Hunger roared inside me. Hunger to bury myself deep in her, hunger to forget everything in her embrace. Hunger to taste her.

I'd never bitten someone like I wanted to bite Carrow. It was depraved. It was wrong.

I did it anyway, giving myself over to the dream.

She clutched my head tightly as I withdrew my mouth from her soft flesh and moved the short distance to the flesh of her inner thigh. My fangs burned to sink inside her, to be enveloped by her flesh. They descended quickly, the hunger roaring inside me.

I didn't hesitate. As soon as I felt the smooth skin of her inner thigh on my lips, I sank my fangs deep into the soft flesh there.

She screamed and bucked, the pleasure tearing through her as I drew deeply at her. The warm rush of blood over my tongue made my head fill with visions of her. Fill with the taste and sound of her.

I could drink her forever, just drown in her.

I ground my hips against the bed, desperate for friction.

"Please, please, please." Her hands tugged at my hair, her voice soft and begging.

Icy terror shot through the dream.

Was I hurting her?

I drew back, fangs retracting, and looked up at her. Desire fogged her eyes and her lips were parted. She tugged on me, pulling me up her body instead of pushing me away.

"Please, Grey. Now. I want you now."

Understanding dawned, and nothing in the world could have torn me away. My sleep trousers were gone in one swift movement, and I fitted myself to her softness, a harsh shudder going through me at the feel of her.

She clutched me close and dragged me to her, unwilling to wait. Unwilling to let this play out slowly as I might have.

I sank into her, so deep that the pleasure shot through my body like lightning. She clutched me close as a shudder ran through me.

Unable to bear it, I buried my head in her neck and rutted like an animal, gripping her hips tight and holding her still for the nearly brutal movements.

She moaned at my ear, holding me tight as I lost myself in her. When the pleasure came, it wrapped hard around me, crashing into me in impossibly huge waves. She followed, gripping me tightly as she cried out.

As soon as it was over, I woke.

Gasping, I stared at the ceiling, my body still hard and my breath still short.

What the hell.

Had that really happened?

It had been so *real.*

The slightest pinch of pain flared at my shoulder, and I reached up, feeling the half-moon indentations of fingernails. Fingernails that were far smaller than my own.

And my sleep trousers were gone. Beneath the sheets, I was entirely nude.

Oh, fates.

That had really happened.

~

Carrow

Early dawn light slanted across my eyes, drawing me from a slumber so deep it felt eternal. I stretched, a yawn abruptly cut off as I remembered the dream from last night.

It had been so damned *real.*

I shot upright, gasping as I yanked off the covers. I still wore my T-shirt, but my underwear was on the ground, torn and tattered. A slight smear of blood decorated my right thigh, and two pin pricks marred the smooth flesh.

Grey's fangs.

Grey had been here last night, and he'd bitten me. Memory of his head between my thighs flashed. He'd done *that* to me.

And I'd loved it. I'd loved all of it. He'd been so much rougher, so much harsher, and more desperate than before.

And I'd *loved* it.

"But it was a dream." I rubbed my forehead, remembering. I'd definitely been asleep, and all the edges had been fuzzy, like a dream. But it had happened. It had really happened. Somehow.

I scrambled out of bed and stood, panting. "Get it together, nerd."

Cordelia appeared in the window. *Whoa lady. It's daytime. Put the full moon away.*

I spun to face her, and she shielded her little eyes.

"Were you here last night?" I demanded.

No, I had a hot date.

"You and me both." I flopped on the bed, unable to believe what had just happened.

Cordelia scampered down and lifted Grey's trousers in one hand and my torn underwear in another. *Clearly. You should write about this and make some money, girl.*

I huffed out a surprised laugh, then sat, my mind whirring. "Grey's trousers are here."

Yep.

He wouldn't have walked home naked. Hell, he wouldn't have come here at all, and certainly not without all his clothing.

"I had a weird dream." I couldn't make sense of *how* it had happened.

You had more than a weird dream.

"Yeah." It had been a little bit like when I'd seen him for the very first time at the scene of the murder that had drawn me into Guild City. He'd appeared in my visions, the first person to do so in a way that allowed him to interact with me.

This had been the same, but different.

Had we reignited the bond?

I tried to feel for it, that powerful connection that linked us together.

I came up empty.

"I don't think we reignited the mate bond," I said. "So we should be safe."

Please let us be safe.

What was it that the blood sorceress had said? I couldn't fall for him? I still hadn't. Last night had been just sex. Well, not *just* sex. But *almost* just sex. It would be okay. Maybe he wouldn't even remember it.

10

CARROW

He totally remembered it. I could see it in his eyes when I spotted him outside of the entrance to Seraphia's library an hour later. He stood next to the door and I was all the way across the street, but his expression was clear as day.

"What's he doing here?" Mac murmured from her spot next to me.

"No idea." *Liar.*

We hadn't agreed to meet, so his arrival was, of course, confusing for Mac.

For me?

No surprise there.

His gaze flickered over me, concern glinting in the

icy depths, warming them. I drew in a deep breath and strode up to him, having no idea what I would say but determined not to hide.

Mac, as if her radar were beeping, lingered back to give us some space.

Grey towered against the small door that led into the library, his gaze on me. Concern etched lines around his mouth and darkened his eyes. "It was real."

I nodded. "It was real."

"I didn't . . ." He dragged a hand through his hair, unable to find words. "I didn't realize. Are you all right?"

"I'm fine." Warmth heated my cheeks.

"Are you sure? I was—"

Rough. Passionate. Desperate.

The words flitted through my mind, but I shoved them away. "I'm fine. Why are you here?"

His brows shot up. "*Why* am I here?"

"Yeah. We should be staying apart. I *want* to be staying apart." *Another lie.*

"You were there, too," he said. "In the dream. So I know that's a lie."

"It was just sex." Even as I said the words, I knew *they* were also a lie. There was no way that could have been *just sex.*

No way in hell.

I met his gaze anyway, pasting my face in hard lines, lips flat and pressed together. "It was just sex, Grey.

Some crazy dream magic. But the bond isn't reignited, so we need to stay away from each other."

He nodded, something unidentifiable in his eyes. "Right. Of course."

"Good. I'm glad we have that settled. I thought it was just a dream, but apparently it wasn't. Now that we know, we won't do it again."

"Agreed." His voice was ice, but that strange look was in his eyes. He said nothing more on the subject, however, and just tilted his head toward the library door. "Good luck in there. Contact me if there is any assistance I can provide." Without waiting for a response, he turned and walked down the street.

I watched him go, the strangest burn in my chest and behind my eyes.

Mac approached to stand at my side. "What was all that about?"

"Hard to explain."

"I can imagine." She studied me, then shook her head. "You'll tell me when you're ready."

If I ever am.

I turned away from Grey, who was disappearing around a corner, and approached the library door.

"It's not meant to open for another twenty minutes." Mac pounded on the door so hard that the ancient wood shook. "Seraphia!"

I went to a small, mullioned glass window and peered inside, gasping at the sight.

Though the exterior of the building was a tiny Tudor shop—no bigger than the Kebab storefront, the interior was enormous. I could only catch shadowed glimpses of it, but the ceiling soared high overhead, and millions of books covered the walls.

Inside, a small, pale figure raced forward. I joined my friend just as Seraphia yanked open the door, looking tired and harried. Her dark hair was a mess around her head, and her eyes were sleepy.

"What the bloody hell are you doing, pounding at this ungodly hour?" Seraphia demanded.

"It's eight forty-five in the morning."

"Oh." Seraphia grimaced. "Really?"

"Are you all right?" I asked.

Seraphia dragged a hand over her face, revealing the glowing tattoo of vines on her forearm. Her dress was well wrinkled and the shadows under her eyes dark. "Please excuse me."

"What's wrong?" Mac demanded.

"Nothing." She opened the door wider to admit us. "Come in. What can I help you with?"

Mac and I shared a glance. That was a brush-off if I'd ever heard one, but we'd only recently become friends with Seraphia. We weren't close enough to push, so we didn't.

I followed Mac into the gorgeous space. Unlike the rest of Guild City, this building appeared to be more modern, though still relatively old.

The interior was grand, reminding me of Notre Dame or St. Paul's Cathedral. But instead of God, this place worshiped books. The enormous space was stuffed to the brim, each soaring wall containing thousands, maybe millions, of tomes on the many shelves. Ornate carvings covered the ceilings and decorated the space between the shelves, creamy marble transformed into scenes from various novels.

There were dragons and knights and queens and witches, heroes and heroines, war and joy. My breath left my body as I spun in a circle, taking it all in.

"Amazing, isn't it?" Seraphia asked.

"Out of this world." I craned my neck to look upward at the domed ceiling. Stars twinkled overhead, somehow visible against the ceiling. It didn't make any sense, but I didn't care.

"What are you here for?" Seraphia asked. "Is it about the kidnappings?"

"It is." I stepped toward her and withdrew the slip of paper from my pocket. Quickly, I unfolded it and showed her the drawing within.

She frowned, studying it. "So you want more information about this image?"

Mac and I nodded.

"Is there anything else you can tell me about it?" she asked.

"No. I know it's an almost impossible task, like finding a needle in a haystack." I frowned, looking at all the books around us. "I don't know how we'll search every one."

"We won't need to." Seraphia turned and gestured for us to follow. "Come, we need to find out where to look first."

I followed her to the middle of the enormous space. Tables and chairs ringed the room, but the center was empty. Tiles had been laid in intricate patterns, their edges blackened by what appeared to be flame.

We were nearly to the center of the room, the shelves towering around us, when Seraphia held out a hand, indicating that we needed to stop. "Wait there."

We did as she instructed, and she strode forward. Silently, she waved an arm over the tiles in front of her, and a green flame burst to life. It flickered and danced, rising twenty feet in the air.

I gasped and stepped back, the heat blasting me. Seraphia chucked the paper into the flame, then waited, her arms crossed.

I watched, awestruck, as the flames died down and smoke curled toward the ceiling. It rose to about fifty feet in the air—only half the way to the ceiling that soared overhead—then turned right, moving horizontally toward some shelves. It zipped down a darkened hallway that I hadn't noticed before.

Seraphia's gaze followed the smoke, and she strode toward it. "Come."

We followed her toward the hallway, entering a

space where the light dimmed to almost nothing and dark smoke curled along the ground.

"No matter what I do, I can't keep this part lit," Seraphia said. "The books just absorb all light."

A chill filled the air, and I shivered. Dark vines grew over the bookcases, some studded with black lilies, and others with thorns.

"I hate this wing," Seraphia muttered from up ahead.

"How is this place real?" I asked, my gaze traveling over the bookshelves that soared nearly fifty feet in the air. The sight gave me vertigo.

"Magic, of course," Seraphia said. "It's connected to libraries all over the world. Like one big library with many secret doors."

"Have you explored it all?" I asked.

She laughed, dodging a spikey vine that reached out for her. "Not even close. There are parts I don't even know exist, I'm sure of it. I can feel them, just out of reach—worlds I've never been to—but I don't know how to get to them."

It was wild. And terrifying.

Finally, she stopped in front of an enormous ladder that stretched all the way to the ceiling. She shoved it over until it was right next to the wispy column of smoke.

Quickly, she climbed the ladder, as graceful as a ballerina on the stage. This *was* her stage, the place she spent her days, surrounded by fabulous books. I liked reading as much as the next gal, but it was nothing compared to the love that Seraphia clearly had.

She retrieved a book and climbed back down, turning to us so that she could hand the book to me. "Your answers should be in there."

The flame and smoke had fully dissipated, leaving no trace. I looked down at it, anticipation singing through me.

"Come." Seraphia gestured for us to follow. "There's a nice table and a good lamp over here."

We left the creepy wing and returned to the main part of the library, which suddenly felt ten times as inviting. She helped us get set up at the table, turning on the lamp so it shone on the ancient book. None of us sat, instead preferring to lean over the book, our gazes rapt. Carefully, I opened the ancient text.

The words were a series of scribbles that I'd never seen before. "That is *not* English."

"It doesn't even look modern," Mac said.

"It's Cuneiform." Surprise flickered in Seraphia's voice and she leaned low over the book. "It's a recording from one of the ancient tablets."

"Cuneiform?" I asked.

"One of the oldest languages known," Seraphia said. "Developed by the Sumerians in Mesopotamia, but it was used over much of the Middle East thousands of years ago."

"Holy fates." Mac frowned at the book. "Why are the kidnappers into Cuneiform? I thought only nerdy old scholars were into it?"

"For the most part, yes." Seraphia leaned closer. "Actually, it looks like a slightly different version of Cuneiform. Perhaps Ugaritic." She gestured to the book. "Keep turning the pages, let's see what it says."

"You can read it?" I asked, hopeful.

"Yes. Not every single word, but most."

"That's some skill," Mac said.

"I've got some weird ones." Seraphia pinned me with an expectant glance. "Now get turning. Let's find that symbol and figure out what the hell is going on."

I did as she asked, carefully turning the pages, and searching for the symbol.

A tiny wisp of smoke seemed to hover over one particular section, so I turned to it, almost immediately finding the same symbol that I'd seen when I'd touched the kidnapper. "Here it is."

Seraphia nudged me aside, clearly excited. She bent over the text and began to read silently. I tapped my foot, anxious to hear what she was learning.

Finally, she looked up, a frown on her face. "The language is Ugaritic, like I thought. This discusses the Temple of Anat at Ugarit."

"I only understood some of those words," I said.

"Right. Of course. You are, in fact, not a nerdy old scholar."

"Sadly, no."

"Well, Ugarit was an ancient Canaanite city on the coast of what is now Syria, right near the Mediterranean. It's really ancient—the first signs of habitation are nearly eight thousand years old. The heyday was about 3,500 years ago, though. Thousands of people lived there until the Sea Peoples destroyed the city in 1190 BCE."

"BCE?" I asked.

"Before Common Era. Same as BC, but in science-speak," she said.

Holy crap that was old. "And the city is still there?"

"It's rubble now, but yes," Seraphia said. "The ruins are still there."

"Isn't Syria in the middle of a civil war?" Mac asked.

"Yes, but I don't think it's active in Ugarit. The city itself wasn't destroyed in the war like some of the other cultural heritage sites, fortunately." Sadness flickered in Seraphia's eyes. "It's rubble only because it is so ancient. But you should be able to find the outlines of the old palaces, houses, libraries, and temples."

"Including the Temple of Anat," I said. "Who was she?"

"She was a goddess of war and peace. Birth and death. She was worshiped in quite a few countries, but Ugarit has a temple dedicated specifically to her. And another to her brother Baal."

"Goddess of war?" I asked, remembering the

crimson magic that had flashed in my mind. It had come with the sounds and smells of war. Had she been trying to contact me?

No, that was crazy. Totally crazy.

But Grey had said my magic was growing.

Was it somehow connecting me to an ancient war goddess? Were they even *real*?

Nope, still crazy. I shouldn't be speculating about that when I needed to be finding my friends. "Our answers have to be at the temple, then."

"Maybe our kidnapping victims, too," Mac said.

Hope flared. "With any luck, yes. We need to go immediately and do recon. We'll pull a rescue mission if it's possible." But how the hell was an ancient war goddess related to this? "Are gods and goddesses real?"

"As real as you or I," Seraphia said. "But they're rarely found on earth, and they are definitely *not* human."

"Neither are we, technically," I said. "There's something a bit different about us, right?"

Mac nodded. "Yes. But we're all basically human, even though we might turn into wolves or cast spells. We're like a different form of human, but the gods . . ."

"They're weird," Seraphia said. "They're all different, of course, but many of them don't have emotions or morals the way we do."

"So we just have to hope this goddess isn't involved, then," I said.

"It's unlikely," Mac said. "If there were a goddess on Earth, we'd know about it. Especially if she was a crazy war goddess who wasn't lying low."

"She wasn't a crazy war goddess," Seraphia said. "Though she had elements of that. She was also the bringer of peace."

"So she was balance," I said.

"That was the idea," Seraphia said.

"Well, we're going to go check out her ruined city," I said. "And pray we don't find her."

"I'm coming," Seraphia said.

"Are you sure?" I frowned. "It's bound to be really dangerous." She could hold her own in a fight pretty well, but Seraphia was a librarian first.

"Can you read Cuneiform?" Seraphia asked.

"Right. Of course not." And there might be clues there. "Please come."

She nodded. "No problem."

"Where are we going?" Eve's breathless voice sounded from behind me, and I turned.

She hurried into the room, her blue dress fluttering as she ran. Today, her hair matched her dress, a brilliant cobalt that gleamed under the lights. Her raven flew behind her, but she paid it no mind.

"We're going to the ancient city of Ugarit, on the Mediterranean coast of Syria," I said. Quickly, I laid out what we'd discovered and what we were going to do.

"I'm coming," she said.

I weighed the pros and cons of more people versus less. If it was just recon, then less was better. If we had a chance at rescuing people, then more was probably better. I just had no idea what we would find when we arrived.

As if she could sense my indecision, Eve said, "You'll need eyes in the sky. I'll take an invisibility potion and fly above the city."

"Do you have any more of those?" I asked. They'd be helpful with recon.

"Unfortunately, I have only one," she said. "They're dreadfully difficult to make."

I nodded. It'd be best if she took it, then. "Air support would be invaluable. Thank you."

She grinned. "No problem. It's the four of us, then."

"I didn't say I was going." Mac quirked a brow.

I laughed. "As if you could resist."

Mac grinned. "So true. But how should we get there? If we don't know what we're walking into, we shouldn't transport right there. We might land right in the middle of something and give ourselves away."

"We could arrive a little way away," I said.

"We don't know what's there or how far spread out they are," Seraphia said. "But I have family on Cyprus. Fishermen. Haven't seen them in years, but they'd take us across the Mediterranean."

My geography was a bit sketchy. I knew that Cyprus

was off the coast of Syria but had no idea how far. "Will that take long?"

She shrugged, then pulled up her phone and consulted something. "Looks like it's rough sixty miles from Cyprus. That shouldn't take more than a few hours by boat, and we don't want to arrive in the daylight anyway."

She had a point. It was still morning, and we'd be best off arriving in the dark. "I like this plan. We can approach from the sea, and Eve can tell us the best place to land. Then we sneak in on foot."

"Exactly," Seraphia said. "I'll just call and see if they'll do it."

"Thank you." I caught her eye and nodded gratefully.

"Anything for a fellow Shadow Guild member." She grinned, then turned to make her phone calls.

I looked at my other friends. "Shall we get ready?"

11

GREY

I left Carrow at the library and walked. At first, I didn't know where I was going. In itself, that was entirely odd.

I was *always* in control.

But now? After last night?

I had no idea what was happening.

When we'd first met, I'd appeared in her visions—right at the scene of the murder that had brought her to my doorstep. We'd spoken, but that was all.

Last night should have been impossible, but it had happened. Something about *us* was dragging us together, even in our dreams. Whether it was fate or her magic or something else, I had no idea.

"Oy, watch out!"

A voice sounded from my left, and I turned to see a bicycle delivery driver headed straight for me. I'd been so lost in my thoughts that I'd crossed the street into his lane.

My gaze met his, and his eyes widened in recognition. Immediately, he veered the bike to avoid me and almost slammed into some rubbish bins.

I shook my head. While it was true that I'd cultivated a fearsome reputation around town, it shouldn't be so bad that a cyclist nearly threw himself into a wall to avoid inconveniencing me when I was in his lane.

And yet, such was life.

I looked up, taking in my surroundings. I'd come to Hellebore Alley without realizing it. Or at least, without consciously realizing it. I needed to be here anyway to hunt down Christoph Venderklein, and that had been my plan for the day, but I'd come here for another reason, I now realized.

Quickly, I strode down the dark street toward Cyrenthia's shop. Surely, she would know what was going wrong. There had to be something I could do about it.

I reached her vine-covered door a moment later and pricked my finger on one of the thorns. As the blood hung suspended over the air, the tiny trap door opened and the goblet appeared, clutched in a hand that didn't look quite as old as it had last time. Rather, it appeared to be middle-aged, at most. Cyrenthia was still thriving from our last offering, apparently.

Still, I pierced my thumb with a fang and let blood pour into the cup. Rules were rules, after all.

The cup retreated, and the little door slammed shut. A moment later, Cyrenthia swung open the door and grinned like a cat, leaning against it as she ran her gaze over me. She looked flawless and young once more, her lips gleaming from the blood she'd just drunk. Though she was leaning right against the blood covered thorns that covered the exterior of her door, she didn't seem to mind.

She raised a brow. "Back so soon, Devil?"

"Yes." My voice was sharp. "There is something wrong with the spell you performed."

"There certainly isn't." She flicked a hand, a gesture indicating I should come forward. "Come, follow me."

She turned and sauntered down the hall, her gauzy, blood-red gown flowing around her. I strode after her, feeling a frown pulling at my lips. She went to the same room as before—it was the only room in her house that I'd seen, despite her efforts to lure me upstairs—and sank gracefully onto one of the modern, black leather couches.

"So." Her red lips pursed. "What has a bee in your bonnet?"

I raised an eyebrow at her choice of phrase.

"Chip on your fang?" she tried.

"The potion that you and Mordaca made—it's not working."

"Yes, it is. I can still see that your fated bond is broken. It's visible in your aura." She tilted her head, studying me. "Though I will say that it's not quite as severed as I would like. I swear I can almost see it trying to return. Fate is a stubborn bitch, isn't she?"

"Then I need help resisting."

"I told you to stay away from her."

"It's not as easy as it sounds." I dragged my hand over my face. "She pulled me to her in a dream."

"Oh." Her lips formed a surprised O. "Really? What kind of dream?"

"There's no need to discuss the details."

"Ah. *That* kind of dream."

"Whatever kind of dream it was, it's impossible to stay away from her when she uses her magic to call me to her."

"I doubt this was entirely her fault." She tapped a crimson nail against her lips.

It was true. I'd wanted to go to her. And from the shocked look on Carrow's face, she hadn't done it intentionally.

"What can you do for me?" I asked. "Because so far, it's not enough."

"I can make you forget her."

Horror struck me. *Forget* her?

I wanted those memories. I *needed* them to see me through the lonely future.

"If you forget her, you cannot love her," Cyrenthia said.

"I don't love." *Her.*

I didn't need to say that last bit because I didn't love *period.* I didn't even know how. I never had, not even before I'd been turned.

"Hmm." She scrunched her nose and tilted her head, a gesture that indicated she didn't believe me. Hell, I wasn't sure if *I* believed me.

"We're working together on something important," I said. "People could die. I can't forget her entirely if we're going to fix that problem."

"I see what you're saying. And you're right. If you forget her entirely, you'll just meet her again and be drawn to her. What I can do is make you forget the romantic past between you. You'll know her and be able to work with her. You'll even know that she is your Cursed Mate—that will help you stay away from her. But you won't remember the sweeter times. You won't feel them pressing on your emotions."

It sounded truly awful. Just the idea of it made my chest feel hollow. But the memory of how I'd felt when the Cursed Mate bond was taking effect was horrifying. I'd felt the old blood lust returning. The curse was so powerful it could compel my will. And it was Carrow's life at risk.

This was no game.

I couldn't be trusted around her.

I nodded. "All right. Do it."

Cyrenthia rose. "This is the right choice."

"It's the only choice."

"That, too." She approached. "Do you have anything of hers?"

"Like a possession? No. Just memories."

"That will have to do." She turned and strode to a shelf, taking a small golden rock from it. Quickly, she returned to me and handed me the stone. "Grip this tight in your hand and think of her. Put a memory directly into it."

She handed it to me, and the stone was cold in my hand—icily so.

Which memory?

Would it be the memory I would give up? No, because I had to give up so many more.

Before I could think too long on it, an image of her flashed into my mind. Her smile as she laughed. The image was so blazing bright that I couldn't get it out of my head.

In my hand, the stone warmed, becoming so hot that it was difficult to hold. I opened my fist at looked down at it, taking in the glowing golden orb.

"Yes, that will do." Cyrenthia plucked the stone from my hand.

I wanted to grab it back, but I tightened my fist, resisting.

She hurried to the large table in the center of the

room and began to work, mixing ingredients and conjuring a tiny fire right on the surface of the table. The little cauldron hovered right over the flames as she stirred, pink smoke wafting from it.

"I'm going to need a drop of your blood," she said.

I approached and pricked my thumb on my fang, savoring the bite of pain that centered my thoughts. I hovered my hand over the cauldron, letting the blood drip. The surface of the potion was a deep red that bubbled when I added my blood. She added hers second, then dropped the small rock into the liquid. Light burst, and a noise cracked loud enough to reverberate against my ear drums.

On the far side of the room, I caught sight of Cordelia. The little raccoon sat in the shadows, watching me with judging eyes. Almost as if she knew what I was doing.

I frowned at her.

It was the only way.

And I didn't *want* to be doing it. I had no choice. Not if I wanted Carrow to survive.

Cyrenthia turned to me and pressed a goblet into my hands. Across the room, Cordelia disappeared.

I stared down at the liquid in the cup, a tightness in my chest that was distinctly unfamiliar.

"Drink," she said.

Like an automaton, I raised the cup to my lips and drank. It burned going down, leaving a trail of dread in its wake. Desperately, I tried to remember things as the potion sought to steal them.

"Don't fight it," Cyrenthia said.

"I'm not.

"You are."

"I can't help it."

She frowned. I drew in a steady breath and forced myself to let the potion take effect. My mind began to fog, memories slipping away like smoke on a breeze.

In their place, emptiness filled me. Sadness, as well —a strange mourning that I'd never felt before.

Carrow.

I could still remember why I was here, but as I thought her name, an emptiness filled me. My chest ached. I struggled not to think of her, not to go hunting for the memories that were gone.

"I'm not sure it worked very well." Cyrenthia frowned deeply, dissatisfaction in her eyes.

"What?" I searched my mind, looking for the positive memories that I knew had once been there. "My memories are gone."

"Yes, but the bond between you is too powerful."

"You broke the mate bond with the other potion."

"I did. And that is still broken. But you've formed a bond without fate's magic, and it is still so strong." Confusion flickered in her eyes. "You really *do* love her, don't you?"

"No. I told you, I cannot love."

She laughed. "I was skeptical before. You're the Devil of Darkvale. Of course you couldn't love. But you *do*."

"I do not." Confusion flickered within me.

"You can lie to yourself all you like, but it's true."

"How can I love her if I don't remember her? It's absurd."

She clucked her tongue. "The heart knows."

"This is ridiculous."

"Well, whatever it is, I suggest that you stay away from her. I don't know that this spell is going to hold very well if you spend much time together. The thing between you two . . . it's just too powerful."

Frustration surged within me, so strong that I wanted to tear something apart. I'd just given up the best memories of my life—though I couldn't remember them, I could *feel* their loss. And it wouldn't even save Carrow?

I said a terse goodbye and left, trying to ignore the strange, aching emptiness in my chest that indicated something enormous was out there, waiting for me.

The day was cool and bright as I stepped out of Cyrenthia's shop. Despite the sun overhead, Hellebore Alley was dark and dreary, as if a shadowy mist hung right at the level of the roofs, blocking the sun.

It suited my mood.

Now that I'd taken care of the issue with Carrow, I had work to do.

Christoph Venderklein lived on this street, according

to Anton. The talent scout for evil, as Carrow had dubbed him.

I rubbed my head, the slightest pain flaring at the thought of her. That memory had remained, but there were so many missing.

For the best.

I reached into my pocket and withdrew the paper Miranda had slipped me on my way out the door. She'd found Christoph's address last night, and now I'd find him.

Though I was tempted to abduct him myself and question him, I doubted I'd get any more information. And it was vital that I did not interrupt any future chain of events. We'd gotten what information we could out of Anton, but we needed much more. Letting things unfold and observing them was the only way to get what we needed.

Quickly, I strode down the quiet street. A few supernaturals were out and about—they'd probably also been out when I'd first arrived, though I'd been in no state to notice them—and they darted out of my way as I passed.

About midway up Hellebore Alley, an even smaller street turned right. Nightshade Lane was damper and darker, smelling foully of wet rodent and body odor. I breathed shallowly as I passed the boarded-up shop windows and checked the walls of the buildings for numbers.

I found Christoph's flat easily. It appeared to be a tiny place right above a long-shuttered butcher shop. A faint golden light glowed from the two small windows, but the angle wasn't quite good enough to see by. I turned and looked up at the building behind me. It was situated right across the street from Christoph's, but the windows were entirely boarded up.

Since I couldn't set up a spy outside of Christoph's flat, I'd have to go with Plan B. Fortunately, I'd come prepared.

I strode across the street and found the street-level entrance to Christoph's flat. It was a rickety old wooden door with a shoddy lock that no one had bothered locking. The door swung open with a creek, and I climbed the narrow, dark stairs to his flat above.

A quick test of his doorknob showed that Christoph did indeed lock his door, but no matter.

I knocked, waiting patiently as I heard footsteps within.

"Who is it?" A creaky voice inquired.

"Open the door." I imbued my voice with my power, and soon after, I heard the doorknob twist.

The door opened silently to reveal a middle-aged man with prematurely stooped shoulders and a mean glint to his eyes. The mage wore clothes far finer than his flat, and I could easily guess how he paid for them.

"Who are you?" Christoph demanded.

"None of your concern." I made sure to put as much

power as I could behind my voice. "You will immediately forget that I am here."

His eyes turned foggy, and I smiled with grim satisfaction.

"Step back from the door," I said.

He did as I commanded, and I walked into the dim little flat. The ceiling was low and the floor sloped, in the way of many of the ancient Tudor buildings in Guild City.

I inspected the small space, looking for the best place to deploy my spying device. There was a dark corner opposite the door that would provide an excellent view of whoever came to the flat in the future.

I turned to Christoph, who watched me with blank eyes. "When Anton makes his requests of you, how does he do it? By note? In person?"

"He sends an intermediary to the door." He nodded at his front door.

"Excellent." It was just as I thought. Anton had always preferred to use minions instead of technology or putting things in writing. It was easier to say someone was lying and kill them than it was to disprove hard evidence.

I withdrew a small charm from my pocket and stuck it to the wall in the corner. It was so small and unobtrusive that it was nearly invisible, but it was the magical equivalent of a video camera.

Satisfied that it was in the right location, I pulled the

corresponding mirror from my pocket and inspected it. The little charm provided the perfect view of the front door and Christoph, standing right in front of it.

Finished, I strode toward the door, stopping to meet Christoph's gaze. "You will immediately forget that I was here, and you will not disturb the charm in the corner."

He nodded, eyes blank, but the gesture full of conviction.

"Good." I turned and left, tucking the mirror back into my pocket.

Christoph shut the door behind me, and I turned back to it, affixing another charm to the upper corner of the door. It clung to the wood using magic, and whenever the door was opened, a corresponding charm in my pocket would vibrate.

Now, all I had to do was wait for Anton's goon to show up. Whoever they chose to kidnap next, we'd know about it and have the drop on them.

12

CARROW

An hour later, Mac, Eve, Seraphia, and I arrived on the sunny shore of Cyprus. Eve's raven wheeled above, stark against the blue sky. Something about that bird...

I shook my head, then looked at the sea. Blue waves crashed against a rocky beach, and the sound of birds cut through the wind. Warm sun shone on my face, and I breathed in deeply. "I need a holiday."

"I could definitely come back here." Mac spun around, taking in the scenery. "It'd be perfect. A little swimming, a little sunbathing . . ."

I joined her, enjoying the dramatic coastline of pale rocks and glittering blue water. Fluffy white clouds filled the sky, and the waves on the ocean glittered under the sun.

I adjusted the bag of potion bombs on my shoulder and looked at Eve. Her eyes were closed as she tilted her head toward the sky, a blissful smile on her face. Seraphia looked tense, however, her jaw clenched and her eyes shadowed.

I frowned at her. "Do you not come home often?"

"Never." She searched our surroundings, her lips tight. "I haven't been back since I was a baby."

I wanted to ask why, but a shout sounded in the distance.

I turned to see an older man and woman approaching. They wore the simple, ancient clothing of fishermen that I'd seen in a Nat Geo documentary and, though they had white hair, their faces glowed with health and strength. The woman carried a basket in one hand and clutched the man's arm with the other as they walked.

"My aunt and uncle," Seraphia said, striding forward to greet them. She still looked tense, but the man and woman appeared to be delighted.

They spoke Greek—or at least, what I assumed was Greek. I'd never actually heard it spoken, despite my fondness for the Greek restaurant that had been located near my old London flat.

Eventually, they turned to us. Seraphia quickly made

the introductions, and I learned that her aunt and uncle were named Aurelia and Stavros.

"Come!" Stavros gestured us forward with a wide sweep of his hands, his accent heavy. "My boat is in the next bay over. I brought it around just a few minutes ago."

"Thank you." I smiled gratefully, and the four of us followed them down the rocky path that led toward the sea.

As we neared, the waves sounded louder, and the scent of the sea grew stronger. I wanted nothing more than to dive into the crystal-clear water, and vowed I'd come back some day.

Finally, we reached the boat that was pulled up on the rocky beach. It was about thirty feet long and had a sloping deck and a tiny cabin near the back. The wood was painted blue and white, and the engine looked ancient.

Were we going to be able to get it off the shore? I'd never seen such a big boat pulled up on the shore like this.

Stavros led us down to the beach. Before I could climb on, Aurelia pressed the basket into my hands. "Food, for the journey."

It was only a few hours, but I wasn't going to turn down food. I smiled and nodded. "Thank you."

I climbed onto the deck, joining Mac and Eve at the

benches in the front. They were built alongside the hull, curving against the railing.

On the shore, Seraphia hugged her aunt goodbye. "Thank you, Aunt. I appreciate this."

"Come home, Seraphia. The land misses you." The woman clutched her arms.

The land?

Mac and I shared a confused glance. That was an odd thing to say.

Darkness flickered across Seraphia's face, but she just nodded and turned, joining us on the deck.

Stavros took up his position at the back and waved his hand in a swirling gesture. Magic flared, and the boat drifted easily back from the beach, floating calmly on the small waves. The engine hadn't even turned on yet.

I waved at Aurelia, who stared at us as Stavros turned the boat to face the horizon. The four of us sat back and watched Cyprus disappear over the horizon. With the breeze and the sunshine, it really did feel like a holiday.

"Let's see what Aunt packed." Seraphia leaned over the basket and opened it, withdrawing various cold salads and a selection of chilled meats and cheeses, along with crusty bread and bottles of sparkling water.

She passed it all around, and we helped ourselves, filling the little plates that Aurelia had included.

"I could get used to this," Mac said.

I grinned and ate, trying to ignore my worry over the people that we were going to save. It would be better to ruminate over plans to save them instead of dwelling on my fear.

We traveled for two hours before the sun began to set. It gleamed brilliant orange on the horizon, the colors bleeding to pinks, reds, and yellows before the sun dipped below the sea.

The air immediately grew cooler, and I wrapped my arms around myself, looking toward the stars. They came out quickly, the night cloudless and bright. Fortunately, the moon was just a sliver.

"We're nearly there," Stavros said. "I can see the shore."

"That's my cue." Eve stood and uncorked a little vial she wore around her neck. As she raised it to her lips, her wings flared behind her, glittering and bright.

She swigged back the potion, a shudder running through her. A moment later, she was gone. I felt her absence more than heard it and, a moment later, her voice whispered out of the comms charm I now wore around my neck.

"Headed to shore," she said.

"We'll await your directions," I confirmed.

Stavros idled the boat off the coast as we waited for Eve to tell us the quietest way to approach. It was only five minutes before she spoke again. "I can sense activity in the city near the temple, also to the south, where there is a human settlement. There's definitely something strange along that coast, as well. Best to avoid it. I think you should approach from the north. Go up the hill, and you'll find the entrance to the city in front of you."

"Is there anyone around there we should look out for?" I asked.

"Just some goats. No shepherd that I can see."

"Thanks. See what you can find out at the city," I said.

"On it." The communication severed.

I looked at Stavros. "Did you get that?"

He nodded, turning on the boat's engine. The engine rumbled almost silently.

I leaned toward Seraphia. "Is he using magic to keep it so quiet?"

She nodded. "Yes."

I stood at the bow with Mac and Seraphia as we approached the rocky shoreline. Tension tightened my skin as the breeze blew the wind back from my face. In the distance, I could barely make out the sight of the city on the hill. As Seraphia had said, it was mostly rubble. Broken walls and tumbled stones, all so ancient that it was hard to believe.

Stavros beached the boat, and we scrambled off. We had transport charms for when it was time to leave, so we waved our thanks, and Seraphia said a quick goodbye. Silently, he drifted out to sea, then turned around and headed back for Cyprus.

The path up the hill was rocky and dusty. I led the way, spotting several goats as I walked. They stared balefully at me as I passed, chewing on some vegetation that couldn't possibly taste very good.

From up ahead, I sensed magic in the air. Something powerful and dark that sent a shiver over my spine.

"I do *not* like whatever is going on up there," Mac whispered from behind me.

"No kidding." I was grateful we hadn't transported right into the middle of it.

Clouds drifted over the moon as we neared the city walls, and gratitude welled. Eve hadn't reported that there were any guards, but it'd be good to have the cover of darkness.

We slowed our pace as we approached the wall, which soared twenty feet over our heads. It was an enormous structure, wider at the base than at the top, with an incline about forty-five degrees. Rubble decorated the top, the remnants of the upper part of the wall.

An arched entryway to the city beckoned us. Whatever wooden gate had once been there was gone, and the tunnel into the city stretched ahead of us.

"Reminds me of the entrance to Guild City," I whispered.

"Only creepier," Mac said.

I nodded, walking silently through the gate. The

tunnel within was pitch black, but I didn't dare use a light. Instead, I walked slowly, my hands outstretched as my eyes gradually adjusted.

At one point, I stumbled. Heart in my throat, I reached out for the wall, bracing myself.

Power slammed into me, my vision going red. Screams echoed in my head, and pain flashed through me. My stomach pitched.

It was that same terrible vision I'd had earlier back in the alley and, again, when Coraline's abductor had touched me.

"Come to me." The voice echoed deep and terrible in my mind. I felt an aching pull dragging me toward it.

Almost immediately, the red turned to white. Calm descended, along with fear. The voice changed, soft and low, whispering, "Resist."

Hands gripped my shoulders and pulled me back.

"Carrow, are you okay?" Mac sounded frantic.

"Yes. Yes." I shook my head. "Just a crazy vision."

"Your magic seems different," she said. "More powerful."

"I don't what's happening, but Anat may be trying to contact me." It sounded crazy.

"Anything is possible," Mac said. "Can you keep going?"

"Of course." I straightened my spine and looked ahead. I could only spot the vaguest shadows and the exit on the other side. From the look of it, we were about halfway through. Magic sparked, vibrant and bright. Torches appeared alongside the tunnel walls, flames sending a golden glow through the space.

"What the hell?" Mac muttered.

"This city is coming alive," Seraphia said. "Some kind of charm, maybe."

Chills ran down my arms as I approached the end of the tunnel. Would there be people? For good measure, I withdrew a stunner potion bomb from my pack and gripped it tightly.

At the tunnel exit, I hesitated, peering out. Mac and Seraphia crowded behind me, also studying the open square at the edge of the city.

"It's empty," Mac murmured.

"But it's reconstructed." The simple, white plaster buildings rose toward the sky, gleaming under the moonlight. There was a slightly hazy look to them, as if they weren't really here, but the entire city looked intact. Albeit slightly transparent.

"We'd have noticed this from the outside," Mac said.

"It was definitely rubble." Seraphia reached forward, as if hoping to feel whatever spell was on the air. "But this is what it once looked like."

"We triggered it when we reached the middle of the entrance tunnel." But *how*, I had no idea. I pressed my comms charm and spoke quietly to Eve, who I could sense above us somewhere in the sky. "Are you seeing what we're seeing? The whole place has come alive."

"I do, yes. Once I lost sight of you in the tunnel, a shadowy image of the old city seemed to appear. I don't see any people, though."

"Not even the ones we seek?" I wish I knew who or how many we were looking for.

"I can still sense them at the temple but can't see them. It's blocked, somehow. More than the other places in the city."

"Which way to get there?" I asked.

"Fastest and safest is to go through the palace on your left. From there, you'll find a path right to the temple. It will lead you through the center of the city."

"Thanks." I turned toward the palace, spotting the enormous wooden doors. They were painted a burnished red to match the straight lines that cut horizontally across the white plaster front.

Mac, Seraphia, and I hurried across the open square toward the palace. It was the largest building in the square, and though it was some kind of royal residence, the architecture wasn't that much more ornate than the other buildings. I quite liked the simple, grand lines of Ugarit.

We climbed the stairs quickly, pulling open the enormous doors and slipping inside a courtyard that was open to the sky above. Beautiful wooden benches lined the walls, and the ghosts of flowering plants stood in the center.

"There are nine courtyards," Eve spoke quietly from

my comms charm. "You should pass by three of them if you go to your right. It's the quickest way to the temple path."

We turned right, heading into one of the large, fabulously appointed rooms. The furniture was simple but large, the gleaming wood draped in colorful fabrics that were slightly hazy. I ran my fingertips over one of them, wondering if they were really there. My hand rubbed over the smooth silk, and I nearly leapt backward, almost surprised to have felt something. I'd have thought it would have felt ghostly—whatever that felt like.

I spun to face Mac. "Are ghosts real?"

She nodded. "Yeah. Not terribly common, though."

"But this place has them," Seraphia said.

"How do you know?" I asked.

She shrugged. "Don't you feel them?"

I supposed I did—a slight chill on the air. The sense of not being alone.

Were ghosts responsible for the kidnapping?

No, that was laughable. It was hard enough to believe in vampires and witches. But ghosts were incorporeal. They couldn't orchestrate a series of international kidnappings.

A pale white figure drifted by the doorway, moving quickly. I started, then lunged toward the door, peering out into the hall.

The figure was gone.

I turned, spotting Seraphia's wide eyes. "That was one of them."

"Didn't want to be seen, though," I said. "Let's keep moving."

We passed through another open courtyard and several more rooms, finally coming to a large office dominated by a desk and chair. A pile of stone tablets was scattered on top.

Seraphia moved quickly toward it, raising her hand and shining a Lightstone ring on the surfaces of the etched stones. She frowned, her gaze darting as she read.

Finally, she looked up, pointing to one of the tablets. "This one is a financial document discussing the costs involved in maintaining the Temple of Anat. Specifically, the upkeep of the attendants."

"Attendants?"

"Her most devout followers kept the Temple in good repair and were responsible for making offerings." She pointed to another tablet. "But this is a letter complaining about the attendants. Costs were getting too high and, worse, the attendants were getting too intense. They were gaining more power amongst the populace, which they shouldn't have been. And they seemed to be gravitating more toward Anat's warlike side, as opposed to the peaceful side."

"So they were throwing off the balance?" I asked.

"Seems like." She frowned and inspected the documents more. "They were a cult, it appears. Trying to pollute the will of Anat and turn the people away from balance."

It was amazing that there were people here thousands of years ago, and yet we were still able to read their letters.

"Get a move on, guys," Eve said. "There's a ghost interested in you. Keeps hovering, and I don't know if it's good or bad."

"You finished?" I asked Seraphia.

"I've read everything." She yanked her phone from her pocket and took some pictures of the tablets. "Let's go."

We left the room and headed through the next courtyard. I swore I caught sight of the ghost again, just the faintest flicker of shimmering white passing by a doorway.

It didn't *feel* evil, but who was I to say?

Finally, we exited the palace and followed a street toward an open plaza. Flat fronted white buildings surrounded the plaza, and I spotted the ghost disappearing into one of the smaller buildings.

I darted after it, determined to figure out what the hell it was doing. It wasn't a threat to us, or it would have already attacked. That meant it could possibly be an ally. Even with Eve in the sky, we could use more help.

"What are you doing?" Mac hissed from behind me.

"Following him." I darted into the little building,

pulling up short at the sight of the shimmering figures all around me.

More ghosts.

They weren't nearly as bright and distinct as the one I was tracking, but they filled the space, sitting around tables. A low hum of energy thrummed in the air, as if they were speaking to each other, but it was impossible to really hear anything.

The figure I'd been following stood behind a long counter. It was far more solid than the others, a simply dressed man in a tunic and trousers. His form was an ethereal white, nearly transparent, though his face was a bit faded, as if he were an old painting.

He didn't run, however.

I raised my hands. "We don't want to hurt you."

He tilted his head to the side.

"Damn." I looked at Eve. "Does he understand me? Can you speak Cuneiform, or whatever this language is?"

"No. I don't know what it would have sounded like."

I turned back to the man. "Do you understand me?"

"Of course." His voice was almost a bit garbled, as if it were passing through magic. I was pretty sure that he was speaking his language, but I was somehow able to understand it. Ghost magic, maybe.

I lowered my hands slowly. "We're not here to hurt you."

He frowned, reaching idly to grip a giant ladle that

protruded from an enormous pot set into the counter. This had to be a restaurant of some kind, or a tavern.

"Do you own this place?" I asked, gesturing to the large space around us. The ceiling was high, with a balcony on one side and windows on the entry wall.

"I do."

"It's very nice. I'm Carrow Burton. Who are you?"

"I am Tarat. Why are you here?"

"We're here about the Temple of Anat. We're having a problem, and we think there are answers there."

He scowled. "Are you one of the newcomers?"

"Newcomers? No. Who are they?"

"Fanatics who appeared earlier this year. They worship the goddess Anat, but not in the way they are meant to."

"Are they modern people?" I prayed they were. It was a hell of a lot easier than figuring out how to fight ghosts or an ancient goddess.

He shrugged. "They're not ghosts."

"Is the Goddess Anat there?" I asked, shivering at the idea.

He shuddered. "She is not, and you'd best pray that she never is. *Never*. She must not rise."

Thank fates. "She's dangerous, then?"

I had felt it in my visions—if that really was her—but I couldn't help asking.

"You cannot imagine."

"Are there prisoners at the temple?" I asked.

"There are."

Hope flared. "Really? They're our friends. We're here to rescue them."

"You cannot reach them. It is impossible. The temple is fortified by the magic of the invaders. No one can pass through. Not even ghosts."

"Who are the invaders?" I shared a frustrated glance with Mac.

"The newcomers who worship the wrong sides of Anat." His form vibrated, frustration evident. "The balance is at risk."

It was the exact same thing he'd said before. I'd clearly gotten all I could out of him. "Will you take us to them?"

"For a price."

"What price?"

"Get rid of them. They have polluted the word and the will of Anat, and they disturb our peace. They are working to bring about a terrible, tragic fate, and you *must* stop them."

13

CARROW

A terrible, tragic fate?

The ghostly figure of the ancient man stared at me, his gaze shadowed. He repeated, "You *must* stop them."

"That's our intention."

He turned. "Come, I will lead you there."

I shared a gaze with my friends, who nodded. Together, the three of us followed him from the tavern and out into the public plaza. It was easier to see the shadows of the ghosts now, though they were still far fainter than the man who led us down the quiet streets. White plaster buildings towered on either side of us, and the thin moon gleamed above.

"How long have they been at the temple?" I asked.

"Permanently? For a month. Though they visited before that." He shook his head. "They were different from the other visitors, however. Too rabid. Too intense. Like wild animals, driven by instinct."

Yikes. I shivered.

Our guide slowed as we neared the dark magic that was thicker on this side of town. It stank, reeking of sewage and rotten meat. He turned and caught my eye. "This is what they are doing to our city. Do you smell it? See it?"

I nodded, my gaze riveted to the dark gray glow ahead of me. It looked like a hazy barrier of smoke separated the temple from the rest of the town. Across an open square, there was a second, unguarded temple.

The guide pointed to it. "That is the temple of Baal, the brother of Anat. They were not interested in it. Only in hers."

"And only in the warlike side," I said.

"Yes. No balance." He shook his head, spitting to the side in disgust. "I will leave you here as there is nothing I can do against the corporeal world. But beware, they have terrible magic. The dark side of Anat may be powering them."

I nodded and tucked myself back behind a wall. My friends joined me. If we leaned around the corner, we could see the open square and the smokey barrier that separated us from the temple. It called to me and repulsed me at the same time.

Our guide disappeared down the street.

I looked at Mac and Seraphia. "How do you want to do this?"

"I say we sneak in and spy," Mac said.

Seraphia nodded, and I had to agree that it was the best way. I touched my comms charm and whispered to Eve. "Can you see into the temple from up there?"

"There are some open-air spaces, but the haze makes it impossible to see the people. I can feel them, though. Like a bunch of rabid skunks making out in a dumpster."

I felt my eyebrows rise. That was quite the visual. "What about a way in? Any entrances look less guarded?"

"Nope, it's all surrounded by the same smokey substance. I think the main entrance is your best bet. They won't be expecting you, at least."

I hoped she was right. "Thanks, Eve."

"I'll stay up here for air support. Just shout if you need help."

"I have a feeling you'll be able to see it before I can shout."

"Probably." She cut the connection, and I peeked around the corner of the building. Everything was quiet and calm. I looked back at Mac and Seraphia. "Let's move quickly to the front, then sneak in and stick to the shadows. We won't make contact until we know what we're up against."

They nodded, and we set off, hurrying across the dark, silent courtyard. The temple itself was as simple and elegant as the rest of the buildings in town, though quite a bit larger. It was partially obscured by the haze, but not so much that I couldn't make out the white plaster and burnished red stripe painted horizontally across the front, about two thirds of the way to the top.

The dark magic barrier pricked against my skin as we approached, but nothing terrible. It was hard to tell where the magic was strongest and where the barrier ended.

"It's not that bad," Mac whispered. "Usually these barriers hurt a hell of a lot more."

I nodded, annoyed by the prickling but not in acute pain. We were nearly to the front steps when the air changed. Pain exploded, and I was slammed backward, feeling like an enormous mallet had slammed into my entire body.

An alarm shrieked through the night air, and I stared upward at the sky, every inch of me ringing with pain. On either side of me, Mac and Seraphia lay still, groaning.

"That was unexpected," Mac said.

"Never seen a barrier like that." Seraphia shoved herself upright. "A real sneak attack."

I followed, aching all over as my heart raced. The

alarm still sounded, a shriek that was surely alerting the people within to our presence.

"Will our transport charm get us out of here?" I demanded, my mind racing with plans as I staggered upright.

Mac stood. "Yes, but do we want them to see us out—"

Five robed figures shot out of the temple, breaking through the misty barrier like it didn't even exit. Their magic preceded them, sounding like war, the clash of swords and cries of pain. It smelled like it, too—blood and smoke and dirt. Their robes were crimson red, with hoods obscuring their faces.

We couldn't run now. We needed to get *some* information at least.

My gaze darted to Seraphia, the smallest and quickest of us. "See if the barrier is open where they came out. They ran through like it was nothing so maybe it has dropped. Mac and I will provide cover."

She nodded, and it was too late to go back.

One of the robed figures raised a hand and hurled a blast of black smoke at us. It thundered like horses' hooves, and through the smoke I spotted an equine nose and galloping legs.

Mac and I dived to the right. As I flew, I took a glancing hit to my legs as the magic blasted by me. Pain radiated outward.

Seraphia darted into the shadows along our left,

clearly intending to sneak around the back of the robed figures who sprinted toward Mac and me.

A bolt of lightning blasted from the sky, hitting the ground between us and our attackers. They slowed, rearing backward. Eve's attack bought us a few precious seconds, allowing Mac and I to rise.

I plunged my hand into the sack of potions at my side and withdrew a stunner, hurling it at the nearest figure. It slammed into his chest, sending him whirling backward, unconscious.

One of his buddies had already powered up another smoke blast, and he hurled it at us. This one was brilliant green and shrieked like a banshee. Mac lunged left, hurling a dagger as she flew through the air. It pierced one of the bastards right in the throat, and he slammed back to the ground.

I darted right, barely avoiding the banshee blast, then dug for another potion bomb. If we could just take these guys out and Seraphia could find the entrance, maybe we'd have a few minutes to sneak in and do some recon before the others realized we'd taken out their partners.

The three remaining red cloaks charged us, their robes flapping ominously on the wind. No matter how fast they ran, their hoods stayed over their faces. They carried ancient swords that looked like something from a museum.

Had they stolen them?

They didn't seem to possess the same long-range magic as the two we'd already taken out.

My hand closed around a third potion bomb and I dug it free, hurling it at the closest one. He was nearly upon me, so close that I could see the shadow of a face beneath his robe. The glass orb smashed against his chest and he went rigid, toppling over.

Behind them, Seraphia was nearly to the part of the temple they'd exited. I prayed she could find the weak spot in the barrier.

Next to me, Mac clashed with one of the robed figures. She punched him in the face so hard his head snapped back, then leveled a kick to his gut that sent him flying.

The fifth was nearly to me, now. No time for a potion bomb. I took a page out of Mac's book and leveled a hard kick at his midsection, feeling a satisfying thud as his sword arm swiped out toward me.

I ducked the blade, taking a slice to the arm that burned like hell. He was off balance, though and tumbled backward.

At that moment, Seraphia reached the barrier and touched it, searching for the opening. The alarm shrieked again, and the barrier blasted her backward, sending her flying ten feet through the air before she slammed to the ground.

"Crap. There *is* no weak spot," Mac cried. Blood

dripped from her cheek, and she clutched at a wound in her side that I hadn't seen her receive.

Damn it, we were in trouble.

The robed figures must be immune to the barrier, or perhaps you could only exit but not enter. Whatever the case was, we couldn't get inside.

"I think more are coming," Eve shouted. "I can cover you with one more bolt, but I'm running low on power."

I looked at Mac, my mind whirring. Three of our attackers were unconscious from potion bombs, but the two wounded ones were rising unsteadily to their feet.

At the temple, a dozen more figures charged out into square. Seraphia still hadn't managed to sit up, either.

Eve's lightning blasted the ground between us and the attackers, the bright light blinding and the noise nearly deafening. It bought us time, though, and I turned to Mac to shout, "We can't take them all. But we can take one back for interrogation."

Mac nodded and dug into her pocket for a transport charm. "You've got your charm?"

"Yeah." We'd each need one if we were both going to carry an unconscious body back. Eve had her own, thank fates. "You get Seraphia. I'll meet you at the Hound."

"Be careful." She darted toward our friend, who was still unconscious. Fear pierced me. *Please be okay.*

I sprinted toward the closest unconscious body. I

didn't need to be grappling with one of the conscious ones, even if they were injured.

The robed figures sprinted down the temple stairs, powering up their magic. It glowed around their hands as I neared the body I'd chosen. I could feel their power in the air, the dark magic that reeked of death and decay. Several of them raised their hands, magic sparking around their palms.

One of them hurled a shrieking green banshee blast right at Mac as she grabbed Seraphia and hauled her upright. It was nearly to them when she slammed her transport charm to the ground and dragged Seraphia into the silvery gray cloud.

They're safe.

Two others aimed at me, magic glowing around their fists.

I was only ten feet from the body. I hurled my transport charm to the ground right next to the still form. Magic flew through the air toward me, two of the smoky galloping stallions. Their hoofbeats reverberated in my chest as I lunged for the body and grabbed an arm, hurling myself into the silvery gray cloud of the transport charm.

One of the beasts followed me in, its magic seeming to pollute the ether that spun me through space. Panic flared as pain enveloped me, threatening to tear me away from the person that I'd grabbed. It felt like I'd been tossed into a blender with a magical stallion from hell. Its hooves slammed into my chest, driving the breath from my lungs.

I clung tight to the arm of my prey, finally tumbling to the ground in the middle of the Haunted Hound.

Panting, I stared at the ceiling. I could feel the arm of the person in my grip, but I had no idea if I'd brought the rest of the body with me.

"Is there a hell stallion in here?" I croaked.

"No missy, but *you* look like hell." An ancient, wrinkled face leaned over me, blue eyes peering hard. "Your boyfriend is wearing a weird outfit, and I'm saying that as a member of the Mystical Mentoria."

I blinked. I had no idea what the Mystical Mentoria was, but the woman did appear to be dressed like a lunatic, in seven different styles of polka dots and a cloak stitched with a million sequins.

What the hell?

Had I screwed up the transport charm?

"Step back, Betty." Quinn's calm voice pierced my panic, and I heaved out a relieved breath.

Betty moved back far enough that I could sit, and I dragged myself upright. In a split second, I absorbed the scene.

I'd gotten my guy—all in one piece.

There was no smoky hell stallion here, thank fates.

Eve appeared, her wings still out and her hair windblown.

And Mac and Seraphia lay on the ground near the fireplace, gasping.

It was about as good as could be expected.

"Who's this bloke?" Quinn asked.

"One of the bastards responsible for kidnapping our friends. He'll come to, soon." I stumbled upright, determined to get to Seraphia, who was still unconscious.

"I'll tie him up then." Quinn bent down and grabbed the body, swinging it up over his shoulder.

I raced to Mac, who was leaning over a prone Seraphia. Eve landed on her knees next to us. "Is she all right?"

Mac pressed her fingertips to Seraphia's neck. "She's got a pulse."

Eve plunged her hand into one of the many pockets of her dress, pulling out a tiny vial. "Healing serum."

She tilted the vial over Seraphia's pale lips and poured the liquid into her mouth.

Nothing happened.

"It always works." Eve scowled.

"What's happening to my plants?" Quinn shouted. "They're all shaking."

I looked up, spotting a few of the potted ferns that decorated the place shaking like they were inside their own personal earthquakes. They tumbled off the shelves and tables and rolled toward Seraphia, the plants clinging to her.

Slowly, the color returned to her cheeks, and she

opened her eyes. The plants stopped shuddering and lay still.

"What's going on?" she asked.

Okay, that was weird.

I shot Mac and Eve a glance. They just shrugged. This power of Seraphia's was new as far as I could tell. Or more likely, it was meant to be a secret.

She looked down at the ferns that were nestled around her, her face going pale again.

Yep. A secret.

"Are you okay?" I asked, ignoring the plants.

Mac and Eve did the same.

"Yeah." She sat up, shoving the plants aside and ignoring them. "There's no way past that barrier."

"We saw," Mac said.

"Did we leave everyone there?" Seraphia asked, worry creasing her brow.

"Not everyone." I stood, turning toward the man that Quinn had bound to the chair near the fire. The patrons of the Haunted Hound didn't pay the scene any mind. Weird stuff happened there all the time. "We got one of theirs to question."

"Good." She looked at us. "Do you think Coraline, Beth, and the rest are okay?"

"I don't think they're dead yet," I said. "They were kidnapped by fanatics of some kind. People with a goal. And they know they're protected inside their temple. I think they'll see their goal out before they kill anyone."

"We need to question him," Mac said.

"First, you need healing drafts." Eve gestured to Mac and me. "Look at the two of you. You look like hell."

Just the reminder made pain flare in my wounds, and Mac winced.

"Here." Eve withdrew two more tiny vials and handed them over.

Mac and I took them, swigging them back quickly. Warmth flowed through me, followed by a wonderful lack of pain.

"Thank you." I smiled gratefully at her.

She nodded, concern still flickering in her eyes. The four of us stood, and we approached the man slumped in the chair. His head nodded on his neck, chin resting on his chest. He was mid-twenties, probably, with shaggy dark hair and a silver bar pierced through his ear. Tattoos decorated his neck, indecipherable swirls that probably meant something to him but nothing to me.

Quinn stood behind his chair, arms crossed over his neck. "You've got to ask him some questions?"

I nodded.

"I've got a truth serum," Eve said.

"I'll wake him up." Quinn grabbed a half-empty cup of water from the table behind him. A red lipstick stain marred the rim. He dumped the water over the guy's head.

The man sputtered and sat up, gasping. As soon as he saw us, he growled and lunged. "Intruders!"

The ropes pulled taut, but he was moving so fast, he upended the chair, tilting forward. Quinn grabbed the back of the chair and yanked it into place. "Chill out, mate."

The man growled and spit, heaving against the bindings.

He was going nuts.

I slapped him across the face, briefly shocking him into silence. Quinn gripped his head and tilted it back. His mouth gaped like a fish's, shock flashing in his eyes.

Quickly, Eve uncorked the vial of truth serum and dumped it into his mouth before he could process what was going on. He sputtered, but most of it appeared to go down his throat.

Quinn leaned close and spoke in a menacing tone against his ear. "Calm down, or I'll gut you like a Ton Ton and climb in for warmth."

I grimaced. "What the hell was that, Quinn?"

He shrugged and smiled. "Been watching a bit of Star Wars."

"Well it's effective," Mac said. "That would get me to shut up."

The prisoner hissed at us, his eyes flashing with rage. "Those potions don't work on me."

Eve frowned. "Who are you?"

"No one you need to know."

"Tell me your name." Her voice hardened.

"Told you, those potions don't work on me."

"Damn it." She turned to us. "He's right. It's not working."

"The goddess protects me," he said. "She'll always protect me."

"Maybe." I nodded, crossing my arms over my chest. "But I bet she can't protect you from the Devil himself."

14

CARROW

Ten minutes later, I dragged our captive down the streets of Guild City. Mac and Eve helped me, each of us taking turns with the wagon we'd gotten from Quinn. Normally it was used to haul kegs. Now it was used to carry our captive. Seraphia had disappeared back to the library, and none of us spoke about the weird episode with the plants.

Behind us, the wagon rumbled over the cobblestones, the body of our captive unconscious inside. In London, you could never get away with something like this. In Guild City, it was a lot easier. We were still trying to avoid the police, but there were far fewer of them, and they didn't really do patrols like human police did.

"Why did your potion bombs work on him but not the truth serum?" I asked Eve, who'd just taken her turn pulling the wagon full of crazy.

She shrugged. "I've heard you can develop an immunity to truth serum if you train. Or he might be protected, like he said."

"It has to be a cult," Mac said. "I mean, look at the robe. They all wore them. And he did sound crazy as a jaybird on Sunday."

I had to agree. I hoped Grey could help us get to the bottom of it with his ability to compel people to speak. If he couldn't, we were almost right back where we started, albeit now with some baggage.

We passed a restaurant with a patio, and the diners leaned out into the sidewalk to inspect the contents of our wagon.

"Just a little performance art," I said.

"Uh-huh." An older woman pursed her crimson lips and nodded, clearly not believing us. All the same, she didn't try to stop us.

We kept going, finally reaching Grey's tower. The shifter guards at the front nodded at me and opened the door, inspecting the unconscious man with bored stares. In the lobby, Miranda looked at us impassively. "What is that?"

"Something we need help with." I nodded toward the back hall. "Is he in?"

"Just a moment." She pressed her comms charm,

never taking her gaze from the unconscious man. Mac and Eve stood by me, idly tapping their fingers against their arms. Miranda murmured into her charm for a moment, then met my gaze. "He'll see you in his office."

His office.

Of course. We were avoiding each other now, so of course he wouldn't invite me into his home. Which was for the best, not only because I came bearing terrible gifts, but also for our future.

We wheeled the wagon back to his office, where a guard stood, leaning against the open door. I wheeled the wagon into the office. Grey sat at his desk and, as soon as I met his eyes, there was something different about him.

"What happened to you?" I demanded, forgetting my friends and our captive and even the edict that we should maintain our distance.

"Carrow." He nodded, his voice strangely cold.

What the hell?

I looked at Mac and Eve to see if they sensed the change, but they were looking at me like I was crazy.

Shit. I needed to get my head in the game. I turned back to Grey, who was suddenly reminding me more and more of the Devil I'd first met. I shoved the thought aside and gestured to the unconscious man. "This is a member of the cult that is kidnapping Guild City's people. He's immune to truth serums, but we were hoping you could use your power to question him."

Grey nodded. "I can try." He gestured to one of the two guards who stood back by the wall. "Get him in a chair."

The two men approached, retrieving the unconscious man, and binding him in a chair. I couldn't take my eyes off Grey as they worked, but he didn't look at me.

"What is it that you would like to know?" he asked, slipping on a thin pair of leather gloves. Why the gloves?

"If the victims are still alive," I said. My bet was that they were, but I needed confirmation so I could stop vibrating with worry. "And if Anat has risen."

"What else?"

I listed off all our questions, and he went to stand in front of the unconscious man, whose chin once again rested on his chest. I'd feel a little bad for him if I didn't know what he'd done. But kidnapping by a cult was the kind of trauma that didn't just go away, and he was partially responsible.

Eve stepped up to the chair. "I have the serum to wake him. Tell me when you're ready."

"Now is fine," he said.

She poured a few drops of a potion on his shoulder, and the man jerked awake, his wild eyes traveling around the room.

Quick as a snake, Grey reached out and gripped the man's chin, forcing him to meet his gaze. *That* was why he put on the gloves. No doubt he didn't want to touch the miserable bastard. As he spoke, power radiated in his voice, making me sway toward him.

I straightened, pulling back.

"Tell me if the kidnapping victims are still alive." His magic made the man's gaze go foggy.

Thank God.

"They're alive." The red cloak's voice was wooden and tense, as if he fought Grey's power. "For now."

"Will you kill them?"

"We won't have to."

I frowned.

"What does that mean?" Grey asked, as if reading my mind.

"They're meant to serve a greater purpose. They will be grateful when it is all through."

Grateful?

I *highly* doubted that.

"Has the goddess Anat risen?" Grey asked.

The man scowled and shook his head. "No. Not yet."

Thank fates.

～

Grey

I stared at the miserable little worm in front of me, working hard to keep my attention off Carrow. Looking at her made my brain feel like it was trying to tear itself in two. I could remember some of our interactions, but the blank spaces in my memory were screaming to be filled. A pounding headache had set up in the spaces where the memories had once resided.

I forced my attention back to the young man who sat in the chair, his chin tilted up defiantly.

Moron.

His voice had turned less wooden though, more passionate. He liked talking about his purpose.

"What's your purpose, exactly?" I asked.

"*Our* purpose. We are the Servants of Anat, and we seek to serve her will."

"So, you're a cult?"

"No, we are servants to the great war goddess herself."

"She is a goddess of balance," Carrow said.

The man scoffed. "Misinterpretation. Her desire is blood and war and destruction."

The fire of bloodlust gleamed in his eyes, and distaste seethed through me. I could all but feel his lust on the air, a slimy film that was exceedingly vile. "No, that is *your* desire. The goddess's true wishes don't seem to factor into this."

His face turned red, and rage filled his eyes.

"What are you doing with the kidnap victims?" I asked, squeezing his chin tight. "What role do they play in all of this?"

He tried to twist his head aside, but I gripped him harder and imbued my voice with all my power. "Tell me."

He spit out the words, unable to help himself. "The ones we've taken all have a purpose. The goddess has many magical skills—each person taken has one of those skills, and they will play a role in the final ceremony."

"What kind of ceremony?" That couldn't be good.

"Ritual killings. For every murder they commit with their power, Anat will regain that magical gift. When all of them are done, she will be powerful enough to rise again."

Well, bloody hell. I believed it was possible. Rituals like this had been performed throughout the breadth of history. If it worked and she returned to earth, no doubt she'd do so as the bloodthirsty half of an otherwise balanced god.

"Why don't you and your friends commit the murders?" I asked. "Surely you're not too squeamish."

"Hardly. We just don't want to die, of course. We need to be here to witness the rise of Anat. To receive our just reward."

"What do you mean, die?" Carrow said. "They're doing the killing, not the dying."

He resisted answering her, so I repeated the questioning.

"The murders must end in suicide," the man said.

"The greater violence will provide the energy that Anat requires to rise again to the earth."

"And you aren't willing to sacrifice your miserable life for your goddess," I said.

"The Goddess Anat *needs* us." His eyes gleamed with passion.

"She doesn't need you. You're a plague." I shook my head, disgusted. "Have any of these murders been committed yet?" I could nearly feel Carrow's desire to have that question answered. Had we lost any of the victims?

"No. They must all be done at the same time. The board is not yet set, but once we have the final piece in place, everything will happen at once."

"It's not a game," I snapped. Carefully, I drew in a breath. My normal icy shell was harder to maintain while staring into the eyes of this lunatic, and it was made harder by my mind's desperate attempt to remember the parts of Carrow that I'd forgotten. "How many more people will you kidnap?"

"One more." He grinned widely, clearly pleased with himself.

"When?" I demanded.

He tried to fight, pressing his lips together, but I gripped his chin tightly, disliking the touch even though I wore my gloves. "When?"

"Tomorrow, we will make the request of Anton. He should find a suitable target that night and, once we have them, we will begin."

So we had a little bit of time. I looked at Carrow, my eyebrows raised. *Anything else?*

"We need you to get us beyond the barrier, into the temple," she said.

I repeated her command, and the little bastard laughed. "I can't. There are only two ways to get in. One of the transport charms given to the kidnappers, or via a lever that temporarily lowers the boundary. But that lever is located inside the temple."

"So you're useless to us," I said.

"I would *never* let you use me against my brethren."

If I were the sort of man to roll my eyes the way the youth did, I would have. Instead, I released his chin and brushed off my hands, rising and turning to face Carrow. Looking directly at her was like looking at the sun during the most beautiful sunrise. Painful, but I wanted to keep doing it.

"Do you have what you need?" I asked.

"For now. We just need to make a plan."

"You'll never beat us," the chained man said.

Carrow turned to him, spitting words. "We will, you little cretin."

She was a glorious, vengeful goddess, and something in my chest swelled. I pressed a hand to it, confused. In pain. I couldn't remember why I liked her so much, but I could feel it. I tightened my jaw and removed my hand, looking at the guards behind me. "Take him to a cell."

The two nodded and approached the cult member, dragging him off. He hissed curses as he was hauled from the room, his robe trailing the ground behind him.

Carrow rubbed her hand over her face. "God, this is a lot."

Instinct surged inside me to get her a chair, food, a drink. Discomfort followed in its wake. Why the hell did I care about that?

Yes, she was supposed to be my mate, but we'd broken that bond. I'd *forgotten* her—or at least, the things that might make me care for her. We should be nothing but acquaintances.

And yet . . .

The instinct remained.

I resisted.

"In a way, this parallels the ancient documents I saw on a desk inside the palace at Ugarit," Carrow said. "The ghostly remains of the palace appeared as soon as we entered and, thousands of years ago, the leaders were dealing with a similar cult who was attempting to pollute the will of Anat."

"Do you think they are the same people?" Eve asked.

Carrow shrugged. "He looked modern to me."

I nodded. "He was not immortal. I would have felt it. I think that the desire to misinterpret the will of a god to serve your own ends is something that never goes out of fashion."

"So we have a modern bunch of psychopaths holed up in a temple about to cause chaos," she said.

"That's what it sounds like." Mac began to pace the room, her short blonde hair growing ever messier as she dragged her hand through it. "We need to get into that temple."

"The only way to do it is with one of those transport charms," Eve said. "Which only Anton's kidnapper will have."

"The security on Anton's casino has doubled, according to my sources," I said. "But I have found his contact in Guild City."

"The evil talent scout who finds the supernatural with the magic that the cult wants?"

"The very same. It's a weaselly mage who lives in Hellebore Alley. I put a charm in his flat that will alert us if Anton contacts him."

Carrow nodded, ideas flickering through her eyes. "We can't get the transport charm from Anton since his place is too heavily guarded. But we can get it from the kidnapper."

"But how do we know where the kidnapper will be?" Eve asked.

Carrow smiled. "We force the talent scout to tell the kidnapper that I'm the target."

Icy fear pierced my chest. "You're suggesting that you become bait."

She nodded. "Yes. They don't know my name. Those miserable weasels have no idea that I was the one to try to break into their temple. They saw me, but it will be Anton's intermediary who tries to kidnap me."

Something roared inside me. *No.* She couldn't take the risk. Pain shot through my head. I rubbed the bridge of my nose, frowning hard. I shouldn't care if she took the risk. She was nothing to me now . . . the spells had seen to it.

And yet . . .

I did care. Incredibly much.

I drew in an unsteady breath, forcing it to move smoothly through my lungs. *I don't like it.*

But I bit back the words. It wasn't my place to like it or not like it. I needed to move forward as if she were no different than anyone else. But it was maddening to still feel the dregs of the emotion while having no memory of the events that had created those feelings.

"I'm not suggesting that the kidnapper *actually* kidnap me," she said. "I'd be totally outnumbered and definitely screwed if he—or she—actually got me. But I'll be the bait and, once he arrives, you guys sweep in and grab him. We'll steal the charm, and then we'll all go to the temple together. Strength in numbers."

"It's the only way," Mac said. "You saw how many of

them there were. If you end up actually kidnapped, it's over for you."

She nodded, her face slightly pale. "You'll make sure that doesn't happen."

I despised this idea.

But it didn't matter.

Carrow looked at me. "You've found Anton's talent scout. Tomorrow, when Anton tells him what magic they are looking for, can you compel the scout to tell Anton that I have it?"

It felt like pulling teeth, but I forced a nod. It was the only reasonable thing to do. And I'd be there to protect her. "Yes."

"Good." Carrow nodded. "We'll figure out the perfect spot for me to hang out tomorrow night so that the kidnapper feels confident approaching, but you guys can be hidden and waiting."

"Then we'll nab the transport charm and break into the temple and save our friends." Eve grinned. "I like this plan."

I still despised it.

"Well, I'd say that's that." Mac brushed off her hands. "We have a plan, and now I need a bath."

"Let's head home," Eve said. "Thank you, Devil."

I nodded stiffly, trying to keep my gaze off Carrow.

Her friends left, but she lingered. Her gaze burned into me, and it was no longer possible to not look at her.

I turned my attention to her face, confusion ricocheting inside me.

I shouldn't want her. I knew all the reasons why, and everything I'd done to prevent it.

And yet I still did. . .

"The other night . . ." Her words trailed off.

Desire flashed through me, the ghost of a memory that I couldn't catch. It left behind the strongest sense of . . . loss.

"The other night," I repeated her words. Should I tell her that I'd wiped my memory? "What about it?"

"What *about* it?" she asked.

I nodded. "What specifically concerns you?"

I hoped that the vague question would lead her into explaining to me what had happened the other night. My heart raced at the thought of what it might have been, like it remembered something I did not. An emotional phantom limb.

"I feel like that should be obvious," she said.

"I don't recall." My words made her eyes flash with hurt and anger. I'd *definitely* said the wrong thing.

"There's no way you don't recall." She frowned at me. "What's going on, Grey?"

"You call me Grey?" The words escaped before I could consider taking them back.

"What the hell happened to you?" she demanded. "You're the ice man again, and there are clearly gaps in your memory."

I nodded stiffly. No point in pretending I hadn't done what I'd done. "I asked Cyrenthia to erase parts of my memory."

"You *what*?"

"I retained the memory that we are—*were*—Cursed Mates. And, also, all memories of our work together on things like this. But it was too dangerous to keep feeling the way that I did about you, so I asked her to erase the good between us. The softer parts. They're gone."

Hurt flickered in her eyes, and she stepped back. "That was . . ." She swallowed hard. "That was smart. Maybe I could do the same."

No.

If she didn't remember, then it would be like it had never happened. Somehow, that felt unbearable.

"It was the safest way," I said, my words weak to my own ears. "I—"

"You don't have to explain yourself." She nodded, her eyes bright. "It was smart. Good thinking."

"Carrow—"

"I'll see you tomorrow." She waved and spun, striding from the room.

I reached out for her, my heart twisting in my chest in the strangest and most unfamiliar way. Seeing my hand stretched out in front of me made me feel lovesick and stupid. I clenched my fist and drew it back.

What the hell had I done?

15

CARROW

I hurried through the dark hallways of Grey's tower, my eyes prickling with tears that I refused to let fall.

Was this all a game to him?

Something he could just toss aside at any time? Erase his memories and chuck it in the bin like it had never existed?

No—it was the opposite. Far from a game, which was why he'd given up the memories. It had been necessary.

Still, I drew in an unsteady breath, pain slicing through me. I knew it was the smart thing for him to have done, but it still hurt, of course.

That dream we'd had...

He doesn't remember the dream.

He doesn't remember any *of it.*

Holy hell, it was all gone for him. Yet I still held onto it, the only one who remembered what had happened. The best night of my life, and I was the only one to remember.

But it was for the best. We were determined to stay away from each other, and we'd done a good job.

Until our magic had dragged us together, our subconsciouses unwilling to stay apart. Fate was so strong—so determined—that we had to fight this with everything we had. Which included erasing our memories.

I was going to do the same.

As soon as this was all over, I was going to Cyrenthia and demand that she erase my memories, too. I couldn't hold onto this alone. I didn't *want* to.

And yet . . . I did.

Finally, I reached the entry foyer. Miranda stood at her desk, her face impassive. Her dark hair was pulled up in a neat knot on top of her head, and her blouse and pencil skirt were perfectly pressed, as usual.

I turned to her. "Does he seem different to you?"

"I'm uncertain what you're referring to?" Her voice was so blandly polite and her expression so passive that I knew something was up.

Miranda and I had not grown *close* exactly, but earlier that week we'd bonded over our worry for Grey. She'd even violated his rules to tell me when he returned from wherever he'd gone. And yet, now . . .

She was as cold as when I'd first met her.

I just nodded. "All right."

She gave me a bland doll's smile, and I turned to leave. The air was fresh and cool as I stepped out into the moonlight. It was dreadfully late at night, and the city was dead silent. Eve and Mac waited for me in the courtyard.

"Well?" Mac raised her eyebrows. "What happened?"

"He forgot me." The words made my chest ache.

"Forgot?" Confusion echoed in Eve's voice.

"A spell of Cyrenthia's."

Mac and Eve's jaws both dropped.

"That's dangerous," Mac said. "The mind doesn't like having holes like that."

"He must have insisted."

At my side, Cordelia appeared. She looked up at me, her little masked face pinched in concern.

I saw it. She wrung her tiny hands. *He did insist. Want me to go have a wee in his shoes?*

It was tempting, that was for sure. But I just shook my head. "Thanks, pal, but no. It really was the smart thing to do, and I'm being silly."

"We should tell the witches what's up," Mac said.

"They'll want to know, and they would provide good backup."

I nodded. "Smart. Let's go do that."

∼

An hour later, after explaining our plan to a group of bloodthirsty witches and coming up with the perfect bait plan, I arrived home as the sun was rising. Mac was in her apartment down below, and Eve had gone to her place just down the street.

I let Cordelia and myself into the little flat just as my stomach grumbled.

Cordelia made a noise of agreement at my side. *You and me both, sister.*

"The kebab place is closed, but there's plenty of snacks in the kitchen."

I'm not sure I'd say plenty.

"You been going a bit wild, lately?"

Depends on how you define wild.

A smile tugged at the corners of my mouth—the first since Grey had told me he'd forgotten me. I should probably start calling him the Devil again. The idea made sadness shoot through me, so I shoved it aside and got to work in the kitchen, unearthing whatever snacks Cordelia hadn't murdered in the last week.

We both gorged ourselves on junk food—something

I would definitely regret later—then fell into bed, she in her favorite chair, and me on the mattress.

I picked up my phone and did the thing I'd been both dreading and anticipating. I sent Grey a text outlining the bait plan, so that he'd know what to tell Christoph Venderklein when Anton finally contacted him.

The message registered that it had sent, and I waited, breath held. It wasn't like his response was actually going to be interesting or make me feel any better, but I couldn't help my desire to hear back from him. For that small bit of contact. For *any* contact.

His message arrived a few minutes later.

Fine.

I stared at it. *Fine.* Just . . . fine.

My disappointment was stupid, of course. And I hated myself for it. For the oddly mooning idiot I'd become. I scowled and shoved the phone away, burying it beneath a pillow.

Grey was doing the right thing by cutting ties and forgetting, and I needed to do the same.

Sleep took a long time coming, but by the time it arrived, so did a shadow at the edge of my consciousness.

Grey.

Like before, I could feel him in my dream, right at the periphery. That time, I'd thought it truly *was* a dream. No consequences.

This time, though?

He was really here. Something about my crazy magic drew him to me, and I wondered if he came willingly, or if I was abducting him.

In bed, I squeezed my eyes shut. I didn't need to open them to know he stood at the edge of my room. I could feel it like I could feel my own legs.

Would he come to me?

Would I let him?

But he didn't *remember* me.

Finally, the tension became too much. I peeked my eyes open the tiniest bit, still cocooned in the partial dream state.

A shadow hovered by the door, tall and broad. I caught the briefest glimpse of cold silver eyes before the shadow retreated, and I was alone.

∿

Grey

The next day, I sat at my desk, staring at an accounts' book but not seeing the figures. My primary goal was to wait for the signal that Anton's man was contacting Christoph Venderklein. Once that happened, I could force Venderklein to give Carrow's name to the kidnapper.

The mere idea of it made me ill, even though I had hardly any memories of her at all. Their loss felt like a severed limb, confusing and terrible.

When I'd chosen this, I knew it was the right thing to do.

But it was terrible.

And this plan . . .

It was so dangerous. But it was smart. Carrow was strong and could take care of herself. She wanted to do this, which meant that I needed to trust her. It wasn't my place to stop her, anyway. And there was no way the kidnapper would risk trying to take me, so I couldn't even trade places.

It will be fine.

The plan was a good one. She'd be surrounded by dozens of people who had her back. The entire Witches' Guild, in fact.

I needed to let go of this stupid concern.

Finally, the damned charm buzzed in my pocket.

Thank fates.

I pulled out the mirror and looked into it, spotting Venderklein standing at the door, speaking to a man with red eyes.

One of Anton's, definitely.

A moment later, Christoph shut the door on the man and turned back to the room, moving toward a coat he'd hung on the peg by the wall. He was getting dressed to go out, no doubt to find the appropriate target for Anton.

It was my cue.

I stood, leaving the room. I nodded at Miranda as I strode out into the afternoon light, turning to head toward Hellebore Alley. It wasn't terribly far from my tower, and by the time I reached it, Christoph was likely out on the street.

I turned down the dark road and moved swiftly past the shops, headed down Nightshade Lane toward Christoph's flat. I was about twenty yards away when I spotted the slender man hurrying toward me, his head bent low.

I ducked into a darkened nook before he saw me, slipping on my leather gloves. I'd have to touch him, and the idea sent a frisson of distaste through me. When he passed, his head was still bent low as he muttered to himself. I reached out and grabbed his arm, yanking him inside.

I clapped a hand over his mouth to silence him, grateful for the glove I wore, and forced his head up so that his gaze met mine. "Do not make a sound."

My magic wrapped around him, making his eyes go blurry and his muscles slightly slack.

"That's it." I removed my hand and propped him up against the wall.

He stared back at me.

"What did Anton's man ask you for?" I asked.

"They want a seer whose gift works by touching objects."

Carrow had that talent. Ice streaked through my veins.

Was it coincidence, or did they really want her? For a moment, I debated changing the plan. I couldn't give him Carrow's name.

I shook myself. *No.* I'd made a promise. And we had a good plan. More than that, Carrow was strong. She would be okay.

I held his haze with my own and spoke, the words feeling like glass in my throat despite the fact that I was honor-bound to say them. "You will tell them that a supernatural named Carrow Burton has that gift. She will be found tonight at an outdoor party at the Witches Guild tower. There will be many opportunities to catch her alone and in the dark."

The words made bile rise in my throat, and I vowed that I would be there to stop the kidnapper before he laid so much as a finger on Carrow.

Christoph nodded. "I will tell them that."

"When do you normally give them a name?"

"Roughly two to three hours after they request it. Doesn't take me long to find a person."

Disgust surged. When this was over, I would beat him to within an inch of his life and evict him from Guild City. He'd sell out his grandmother for a cigarette, and I didn't want his kind here. "You are truly the dregs of the gene pool."

Irritation flickered in the man's eyes, and I raised a hand to his neck, gripping it. The desire to crush his windpipe was strong—too strong.

I drew in a steadying breath, knowing that I was teetering at the edge of something here. I'd lost my memories of Carrow, and it had left me unsettled. Angry and always on the edge.

"In two hours, tell Anton to send his goon after Carrow." I shook him slightly. "Do not deviate from those orders."

His eyes had properly blurred, indicating the effectiveness of my power, and I nodded, releasing him. "Now go. Walk around town as if you are doing your normal business, then return home and do as I have commanded."

He nodded and turned, striding out into the street. His stooped posture remained the same, and I watched him head down the road as if he were continuing on his way. I'd need to keep an eye on his apartment to make sure he did as I said, but it was clear he would not disobey me.

I pulled my phone from my pocket to send a message to Carrow, hesitating just briefly.

I could go tell her in person.

Desire pulled me toward that option, fueled by the need to see her.

No.

I couldn't. Cyrenthia had been clear. We needed to stay apart.

I typed the message and hit send.

16

CARROW

That night, Mac, Seraphia, Eve, and I sauntered down the street to the Witches' Guild party. It was a truly last-minute affair, the idea cooked up less than twenty-four hours ago. As expected, Guild City had responded quickly.

Only the witches knew that it was a trap for the kidnapper, but everyone else liked a good party, and the witches threw the best. I hadn't yet seen Grey, but I knew he'd be there.

The sound of the party echoed through the clear night as we neared, shouts and laughter sounding down the quiet, cobbled streets of Guild City. On the horizon,

I could see the colorful sky lit up with magic, marking the spot where the festivities were meant to go down.

If this didn't work . . .

"We're screwed if this doesn't work, aren't we?" I asked.

Seraphia nodded. "I've been reading more about the goddess Anat, and you were right, their actions parallel those of cults in the past. They seem to be obsessed with her."

"Ritual murders, though?" Eve shook her head, a disgusted expression on her face.

Her raven made a harsh noise of agreement, but she didn't seem to hear it.

"We're lucky they've been collecting people for one big event and didn't start piecemeal with individual murders," Seraphia said.

"Like it's all some horrible game, and they're setting up the board," I said. Was I the last piece? The fact that they wanted someone with my power made me seriously nervous. I shivered. "They want to make a splash."

"Exactly," Seraphia said. "They'll imbue her with power that satisfies her dark side, so when she rises, there will be no balance."

"We'll stop them." I stepped out into the courtyard that surrounded the Witches' Guild tower.

The space that was normally so barren and desolate was filled with life now. Dozens of supernaturals drank and danced and talked. Part of the wild grass had been covered by sand, and palm trees grew up out of the golden stuff. Bonfires scattered the space, brilliant orange infernos emitting colorful smoke that hovered over the guests like an Aurora Borealis. Picnic tables and games were set up, along with what looked like a match of American football, complete with a line of cheerleaders, both men and women.

"This is wild." I took it all in, amazed by what the witches had accomplished in such a short time.

"Look at all the little nooks they've created." Mac nodded toward the edges of the courtyard.

As planned, there were quiet spaces set away from the masses of people. In the shadows of the abandoned shops were benches under palm trees and blankets spread out on the grass. People already inhabited half of them, talking and flirting.

I eyed the one in the far corner that we planned for me to inhabit, eventually. It was quiet and secluded, near a little nook between two shops. A couple of alleys were located nearby, along with a segment of flat roofs that the kidnapper could hide on. We were betting that he would, in fact.

Eve gestured subtly toward the spot. "Yours is ready, just like we planned."

I nodded, going over it in my head. We'd concocted it last night with the witches, and now it was time to put the plan into action. I was meant to spend at least two hours "partying" and appearing to grow more drunk. Eventually, I'd wander off to the shadowed corner spot to have a break, and maybe pretend to vomit. It was quiet and secluded enough that the bastard could grab me in a heartbeat and transport me away.

If we weren't prepared.

But we were.

Massively so.

There were nearly three dozen witches scattered about, ready to fight, along with my group. Not to mention myself. No way in hell I'd let him take me.

"Let's get this party started." I strode forward, a big grin on my face.

Adrenaline raced through my veins as I approached one of the many kegs set into massive ice buckets at the base of the house. Mary stood next to them, grinning wildly and filling beers as quickly as people passed their red plastic cups.

I neared, and Mary smiled with a manic expression on her face. Her pink eyes were serious, though, if one knew to look. It was all an act.

"Hey, Mary."

"Carrow!" She shrieked her excitement, putting on a good show for the kidnapper if he was watching. "We've themed it after an American college party."

My gaze moved to the kegs. "Is that what these are all about?"

"Yep!" She discarded the tap hose from one keg and

reached for another. "You have to try this one, it's fantastic."

She filled a glass and I took it, taking a deep sip.

Disgusting.

I barely resisted spitting it out.

I'd heard that non-alcoholic beer wasn't any good, and boy, did this prove it. I swallowed and gave her a big grin. "It's great, thanks."

Her magenta eyes twinkled with knowing mirth. "Yeah, it's the actual worst, isn't it?"

We were surrounded only by witches and my friends, so I was able to speak truthfully. "Yep."

"Bottoms up!" She grinned and swigged back her own cup, masterfully suppressing a grimace.

The whole point of the party was to make me look like a drunken idiot, easy prey. If everyone else looked like drunken idiots, too, it was even better. Frankly, the witches had nailed it on the theming. The kidnapper would think it was a walk in the park.

Eve, Seraphia, and Mac each accepted a cup of the terrible beer, and Mary pointed to the collection of tables set up in the middle of the courtyard. "Drinking games are over there. Get to it."

"Thanks." I gave her a nod and departed, my friends at my side.

Every minute, more people flowed into the party. The noise and energy vibrated through the place, and I looked around, searching for Grey.

He was there. I could feel it. I could feel *him*.

But where, I had no idea. I knew I could count on him being nearby when I staggered over to Kidnappers Corner, though.

The thought made me feel better.

We neared the tables that were set up with various red plastic cups in different arrays, people spread out around the tables and cheering as the games progressed. There was a lot of chanting and a whole lot of spilled beer.

The witches were insane geniuses.

"Let's play some Flip Cup," Mac said.

"What's that?" I asked.

She pointed to a table where cups were positioned upside down on either edge, partially hanging over the side. "It's that one right there. I learned about it on Google when the witches wanted help planning the party. Apparently, we have to flip cups over, and if we don't do a good enough job, we have to drink."

"Sounds like a blast."

We joined a group around a table and started playing. Despite the stress of the situation, it actually was pretty fun.

Mary joined us at one point. Music blared over the loudspeakers that I couldn't see, some kind of enthusiastic chanting that I didn't recognize.

"What's the music?" I asked her.

"College football theme songs, or something." Mary

shrugged. "You know, the game with the big blokes who hit each other, not proper football."

As the music played, the chants changed in tone and phrase. *Rock Chalk Jayhawk*, *Roll Tide*, and *Glory Glory to Old Georgia* buffeted up against *Boomer Sooner*, *Rocky Top*, and *Woo Pig Sooie*.

Mary must have caught my baffled expression and said, "I have literally no idea. We basically stole every American college thing we could find and smashed it together to make this party."

As weird as it all sounded, everyone seemed to be having a damned good time. Especially the people drinking the real beer.

We turned our attention back to the games and continued playing. As I flipped cups and tossed Ping Pong balls and sandbags at their targets, I drank more and more fake beer. So did my friends, and soon we were all pretending to move a little more awkwardly and trip a little more often.

I could feel Grey's gaze on me the entire time, burning across my skin in a way that sent shivers down my spine. I ignored it as best I could and focused on building the charade.

Finally, it was time. The crowd was dense and pissed, the sober witches having moved strategically to the edges of the crush so that they could be nearby when shit went down. Some of them danced and breathed fire in a fantastic display, while others "drunkenly" hula-hooped around the open spaces in the courtyard.

All were ready for action.

I turned to Mac. "I'm out of here. Need some air."

She nodded, her expression concerned.

"Try to look more pissed," I muttered. "You're looking sober and scared."

"Alright, mate." Her expression changed, going slightly slack.

"Good job. See you soon." I staggered through the crowd, clutching my stomach like I was going to be ill. When a particularly large crush of people surrounded me, I reached into my pocket for the small stunner bomb that Eve had given me. I also wore some heavy jewelry fitted with useful potions—*just-in-case* potions— but hopefully I wouldn't need them.

With the potion bomb trapped under the palm that I'd pressed to my stomach, I was ready. And yet, the crowd was just so damned thick.

"I'm going to be ill," I said, just loud enough for those around me to hear.

It did the trick, and the masses parted for me, letting me escape into the fresh air. The quiet nooks set away from the party were still only half full. Most people had been seduced into the action by the games and crazy music, and the setting was just right for our trap.

My senses were on high alert as I stumbled toward the quiet corner farthest from the party, hoping that I wasn't laying it on too thick. I could feel the eyes of someone watching me, and I was almost entirely certain it wasn't Grey.

The kidnapper.

The close attention felt cold and clammy, not warm and lovely, the way Grey's felt.

I reached the bench and flopped onto it, the potion bomb clutched in my hand. Every hair on my body stood on end as I waited. If this guy was anything like the last, he'd be fast and powerful.

As I sat, I could feel Grey's gaze on me, as well. Everyone else was ignoring me—or so it seemed. I could feel their attention just as strongly, even though they weren't looking at me.

When the kidnapper appeared behind me, I sensed it. A slight change to the air, like a prickle of magic that stung my skin. The scent of burning tires preceded him, his dark magic impossible to hide. The sound of crunching gravel sounded only a few feet behind me.

I leapt up and spun around, heart hammering.

The red-eyed bastard stood right behind the bench, his huge shoulders slightly hunched and his mouth twisted into a permanent grimace. Shock flashed in his eyes, and I hurled the potion bomb right at his chest.

It bounced off as if there were a barrier surrounding him, slamming to the ground and exploding.

What the hell?

He lunged for me, and I darted backward, fear icing my skin.

Magic surged on the air, and lightning struck from above. It shot downward from the flying figure who hovered right overhead—Eve. The bolt aimed true, slamming into the man's head, cracking and bright.

He didn't so much as flinch—just leapt over the bench and grabbed for me. I ducked, darting to the side to avoid his grasp.

From behind, a dozen blasts of magic shot through the air. They slammed into the man, a rainbow of different attack spells conjured by the witches.

Horror dawned as every single one bounced off him. One slammed right into me, turning my knees into jelly as I slammed to the ground, suddenly weak.

Through bleary eyes, I spotted a glowing charm around the kidnapper's neck. Was that what was protecting him?

Conflicting desires surged within me—*run* and *attack*. But we'd never have another chance.

If only I could get that necklace . . .

The kidnapper lumbered toward me, rage in his eyes. He was determined to finish the job now that it had started, and the attack had just pissed him off.

As I scrambled to my feet, Grey appeared at the corner of my vision. He hurtled toward the kidnapper, as fast and powerful as a train. In seconds, he'd reached the hulking brute. He grabbed for him, but the protective shield around the bastard blew Grey backward.

He was prepared this time. Though he flew ten feet through the air, he landed in a graceful roll and popped up to his feet, ready to charge again. Behind him, the witches and my friends were converging, magic glowing around them as they readied themselves to strike.

Yet, it wouldn't work.

I was the only one who could possibly get to him since he wanted to catch me. I drew my dagger and lunged for him, so close that I could see the scowl lines dug deep into his face.

I raised the blade, drawing his attention to the gleaming steal. He was distracted just long enough that I could swipe out with my free hand and yank the charm from around his neck.

A blast of magic shot from the sky above, slamming into his head. He went to his knees, his roar of pain echoing in the night. I planted my dagger into his shoulder, but he was too fast. He swiped out with a massive fist, slamming it into my face.

Pain exploded through my skull, my vision blackening as my legs weakened. A strong arm grabbed me around the waist, and the painful magic that shot through me made it clear that it wasn't a friend who'd grabbed me.

Through flickering vision, I caught sight of Grey. He was nearly to us, fear in his eyes and rage twisting his mouth. An explosion of orange powder sent fear racing though me.

The transport charm.

I felt the ether suck me in right as Grey arrived. He followed us into the ether, the party disappeared from behind him, replaced only by black. His hand grazed my arm as he tried to grab me away from the kidnapper, but the ether was stronger, yanking us through and spinning us away.

I nearly blacked out, the pain and pull of the ether too much. When the ether spit us out at Ugarit, the kidnapper chucked me to the ground. I landed hard, pain singing through my shoulder. Weakness pulled at every muscle, and I just lay there, eyes slitted.

Well, shit.

I'd been kidnapped.

And Grey wasn't here. I'd feel him.

I'd known this was a possibility, but thought it highly unlikely, considering the fact that we had the entire witches' coven on our side. I'd underestimated Anton's goon, though.

This was better than nothing, though. At least I'd be on the inside.

"I'm here," the bastard bellowed.

I played dead, pretending to be unconscious. Through narrowed eyes, I could see that we were in the middle of an open courtyard inside the temple. The protective dome shimmered overhead.

From the other side of the courtyard, five red-cloaked figures appeared. Their faces were all blocked by their hoods, but the magic radiating from them felt slimy and gross. Behind them, I could see dozens of figures appear through doorways and windows.

There were so many of them. We'd need an army to take them all.

Fear slithered down my spine.

Don't think of it.

I needed to focus on my goals—rescue those who had been kidnapped and find that damned lever to let my friends in.

The figures neared. One of them paid careful attention to me, his frank perusal making my stomach turn.

"She's conscious." He raised a hand and shot a blast of red magic at me.

Pain slammed into my head, and darkness took me.

Minutes or hours passed—I had no idea—but I felt him again.

Grey.

Just like in my dreams.

My mind was foggy, but I fought to remember what was going on. Why was I asleep right now?

Kidnapped.

My friends were back at the Witches' Guild and I was here.

"Grey," I shouted, the words sounding hollow in my mind. But I could feel him.

Grey.

I called upon my magic, trying to manipulate it to my will. It had been growing, connecting me to him, and maybe even to the voice in my head that I thought might be Anat. I just needed to make my magic do what *I* wanted it to do.

I envisioned him, trying to find him through the ether. Trying to go to him in whatever strange and magical way that I could. He was so close, I just needed to get to him.

17

GREY

I reached for Carrow, but she slipped through my grasp. The ether pulled her away and spat me out, shoving me back into Guild City. I slammed to the ground, terror racing through me.

Heart thundering, I surged to my feet and searched the area around the clearing, desperate to find her.

Of course she wasn't there.

My skin turned icy. I'd never felt such fear in all my days—not even when the vampire had turned me so long ago.

They'd taken her.

The fear blasted through my mind, a tornado that

cleared away the cobwebs. Memories of her surged to the surface, crowding out everything else. They'd been lost only a day ago, yet it felt like they'd been gone forever.

Now I could recall them all. Cyrenthia's spell was breaking, and every moment I'd spent with Carrow was unearthing from my mind.

I nearly went to my knees.

How had I gotten rid of these? How had I borne it?

And she was gone.

A voice sounded in the distance, and I felt the party receding. The music and shouts all drifted away, my surroundings turning shadowed.

"Grey," Carrow shouted.

I spun around, searching for her. But all I could see was darkness. Stone walls. My eyes adjusted, taking advantage of the thin sliver of light that turned the space from black to gray.

I stood in a cell, a lump at my feet. My chest felt strange—different. My heart raced.

"Carrow." Fear pierced me. I fell to my knees, reaching for her. My hands passed right through. "Why can't I touch you?"

She blinked up at me, dazed. "I don't know. Maybe the spell on the temple."

"They've taken you to the temple?" I reached again for the ropes around her wrists, but my hands passed through.

"Yes. I think I've called you here with my magic."

I nodded. "You did."

"Wild." She swallowed hard, clearly in pain. What had they hit her with? "You need to bring everyone you can to the temple. I've seen dozens of cult members, and we're going to need an army to fight them."

"I'll bring one."

"Good. Get here and wait silently. In shadows. Don't just burst in. I need to get out of this cell and find the lever that will disable the magical barrier that protects the temple."

How the hell was I supposed to wait quietly while she was in here, tied up?

As if she could read my thoughts, she said, "You *must* do this as I say. There are so many of them. If you show up here and try to break your way in, they'll have warning, and they could start the ritual. I was the last person they needed, remember?"

She was right. I nodded. "I'll bring an army, and we'll wait in the shadows until the protection on the temple drops."

"Perfect." Her gaze moved to mine. "Now go. This will work, I promise."

I wanted to reach for her again, but her magic shoved me backward, out of this half world and back to the Witches' Guild.

I swallowed my fear and rubbed my chest. What the hell had just happened?

I'd been called to Carrow, but something else had happened.

The mate bond.

The spell that Cyrenthia had cast to break our mate bond was fading. I could feel the fated connection growing, fighting past the blood sorceress's magic. Every time Carrow called me to her, it must fade a little bit.

I couldn't think about it now.

I turned back to the party, spotting nearly forty witches nearby, standing in a semi-circle, shock on their faces. Mac and Seraphia pushed through the crowd, their faces white.

"They got her." Mac's wide eyes searched the area that was now empty.

"I saw her," I said. "She called me to her with her magic."

Mac's brows rose. "Whoa. Her power is really growing. What did she tell you?"

I laid out the plan, quickly and concisely. I wanted to storm that temple and take it by force, tearing the throats out of anyone who stood in my way. I forced away the desire.

"Okay," Mac said. "So we go now and set up. We'll be there waiting when the barrier drops."

Mary stepped forward, nodding. "The witches will be ready in ten minutes. A little longer to get a proper portal set up. We're too many people to use transport charms."

I looked at the figures standing in a semi-circle around us. It was the army I'd promised. With my security forces, we'd have enough. I just prayed that this would work.

~

Carrow

Consciousness came in fits and spurts, my head aching like it had been hit with a giant mallet. Though my vision was still bleary, my other senses were working fine.

I'd just called Grey to me in my dreams. I rubbed my chest. What the hell was that feeling? Almost like our mate bond was trying to return.

We were supposed to stay apart, yet I kept calling to him in my sleep. Fate didn't care if I did it unconsciously.

No time to think of it now.

Grey was coming with an army, and I needed to find the lever and drop the barrier on the temple.

Carefully, I drew in a breath, focusing on my surroundings.

I lay bound on a cold, hard floor, my wrists tied in front of me and my head flopped on the ground. It smelled of the sea and ancient stone, but there was almost no noise. Blinking, I took in the small white room.

My magic felt blocked, no doubt by a spell cast on the room, but I was still wearing the jewelry that Eve and the Fae dress shop owner had created. There were a variety of useful potions stored in the wide cuff bracelets, and they were definitely going to come in handy.

Aching, I sat up.

Cordelia appeared next to me, the little raccoon wringing her tiny hands as her worried eyes inspected me. *You got nabbed.*

"Yep." I rubbed my aching head and looked around.

I was alone with no sight of the other prisoners, but at least there were no guards watching me.

I thrust my wrists toward her. "Little help, please?"

She nodded and got to work, moving quickly as she tugged at the knots. It took her a few moments, but finally the bindings fell free.

Want me to go scout the hall?

"Genius. Thanks, Cordelia."

She shook her head. *This was a dumb plan.*

"It was our only option."

Yeah, yeah. She disappeared.

I stood, facing the door. There was a little window in it, and I hurried up to it and peered out warily. There were only a few torches affixed to the walls, giving off a faint glow that barely illuminated the dark corridor.

Several more doors dotted the hallway. Each had a little window in it, and I wondered if the temple had originally had cells built into it or if these rooms had been re-purposed from something else.

Across the hall, a face appeared in the little window set into the opposite door. Dark eyes and golden skin, along with straight black hair.

"Coraline!" I whispered.

"Shh." Her eyes darted left and right, then her expression relaxed. "The guards are gone, thank fates. Did they get you, too?"

I nodded. "Yeah. But help is coming. I was bait, and it went wrong."

Coraline's brows rose. "Bait? That's quite bold."

"We couldn't get into the temple otherwise."

She nodded, a knowing look in her eyes. "The shield. I know. It's powerful. Is my coven coming?"

"Yes. If I can get out and pull the lever to drop the shield that protects this place. How many other prisoners are there?"

"At least a dozen."

"A *dozen*?" It was so many more than I'd expected. They must have been taking supernaturals from other towns as well, maybe organized through someone other than Anton.

Cordelia appeared at my feet. *Coast is clear out there. No one in any of the nearby halls. Lots of prisoners, though. Each locked in their own room.*

"Thanks, pal." I looked back up at the witch on the other side of the hall. "Give me a moment, and I'll get us out of here."

She nodded, and I ducked behind the door and fumbled in the wrist cuff for a tiny vial of magical acid-like substance that would melt the metal. When Eve had given me these bracelets prior to the party, she'd explained what each of them did.

We had hoped I wouldn't need them, but we both knew it was a possibility.

The tiny vial glowed yellow between my fingertips. I uncorked it and poured a tiny amount onto the metal lock. I was stingy with it, wanting to preserve as much as possible to help get Coraline out. There was no way I'd have enough to free everyone, but I'd cross that bridge when I came to it.

The lock sizzled, a tiny cloud of green smoke billowing outward. When the smoke settled, I pulled on the door. It stuck for a moment, then broke open.

Across the hall, the witch grinned at me. "Nice."

"I've got a little more. Step back."

She disappeared from the window, and Cordelia and I hurried across the hall. I poured the rest of the potion onto the lock and watched it smoke and sizzle. When it was done, I pushed hard on the door.

It popped open, and Coraline rushed out. She was still wearing the crazy feathered outfit that she'd been abducted in, but the plumes were all broken and dirty now. She flung her arms around me. "You rock, Carrow."

I hugged her back, then pulled away. "We have reinforcements coming—including your coven—but we need to disable the barrier that protects the temple. There's supposed to be a lever that will drop the protective shield. Do you know where it is?"

"No, but I know some places it's not. Areas where the weirdos congregate."

"We'll want to avoid those." I crossed the hall and shut my door, so it looked like I was still inside. She did the same to her door. "Let's go find it."

"What about us?" A voice whispered.

"We'll get you out, Beth," Coraline whispered. "Promise."

"Beth's over there?" I hurried to the door and looked through the window.

A woman sat against the wall, looking exhausted and too skinny. Her midnight braids hung down her back, threaded through with beautiful emerald silk that sparkled despite the dim light. She surged upright. "Carrow!"

"Beth. We've been looking for you." I fumbled in my bracelet for another one of the potions that would melt the lock. I only had two more, and I needed to save one in case the lever was behind a locked door. But I could get Beth out at least.

When I looked back up, she'd come to stand at the window. I handed her the potion. "Just use half, and you can use the other half to let someone else out."

Coraline shook her head. "We don't want to alert them that something is amiss. There are over a hundred people in this crazy cult, and if they know we're out, we're screwed."

Beth nodded. "She's right. I'll hang onto this potion and stay here. If the guards show up, I'll create a ruckus to keep them from noticing you're gone."

"Thank you."

Cordelia's tiny hand tugged at my leg. I looked down.

If the prisoners hold me up to their lock, I can pick it. She held up two tiny pieces of metal.

I raised my brows. "That's handy."

Very.

I looked up at Beth. "How do you feel about raccoons?"

"Fantastic." She said. "Is Cordelia here?"

I nodded and explained about the locks and her skills.

She nodded. "All right. I'll tell the other prisoners not to freak out when a raccoon appears in their cell."

Cordelia scoffed. *Freak out? Rude.*

I rubbed her head. "You've got this, pal. Thanks."

She nodded, and I left her to it. Coraline joined me, and I gave her one of my two daggers. "Just in case."

"Thanks." She grinned and gripped it tight.

We hurried down the hall, passing the cells. The prisoners watched us silently from behind their tiny cell windows. Some of them had heard the exchange with Beth, and whispers were traveling down the hall as each person alerted the room next to them.

"Good luck," one woman said, and a new wave of fear clutched me.

What if we were too slow? What if we couldn't find the lever. If we failed these people . . .

I shook the thought away.

We reached the end of the hall, and Coraline gestured to the left. "This way. Guard quarters to the right."

I followed her left, and we slipped down another hallway. Immediately, I felt the spell that had suppressed my magic fade.

Coraline sighed softly, moving her shoulders in a stretch. "That's feels good. I hated that spell."

"Let's work our way methodically through the temple. We have to find the lever eventually."

"We can do that. It's roughly rectangular, I think. We'll work our way around counter-clockwise."

"How do you know your way around?"

"We're taken out occasionally for 'training'." She put air quotes around the word. "They're trying to brain-wash us to perform some horrible ritual, but it's not working."

"That's good, at least."

She shook her head. "For now, maybe. But I think they're trying to come up with a potion that will force us to do their bidding."

I grimaced. Shit. "Doesn't matter. We're getting out of here tonight and putting an end to all of this."

She nodded. "I'm going to kill every bastard I see."

We crossed through a large room that was filled with a shallow pool. Torches gleamed along the walls, shedding a warm, golden light on the glittering water. Golden fish swam over the pale blue tiles. Benches surrounded the pool, and I couldn't believe how big this place was. "It's a maze."

"It's enormous. I've already seen so many rooms, I can't keep track."

A dark red line was painted on the ground through the middle of the room, cutting right through the shallow pool. We'd seen a similar line painted through the hallway, as well. The paint was messier than the rest of the tidy temple. I pointed to it. "What's that? It doesn't look like it was built into the place but added later."

"No idea. But I've seen them everywhere. If you hover your hand over it, you can feel magic."

I ducked low and did as she said, feeling the buzz of magic. "Weird."

We were nearing the door when a noise sounded from up ahead, the scrape of shoes on the floor.

I darted to the wall, tucking myself beside the door. Coraline hid on the other side. She held her dagger up, a bloodthirsty gleam in her eye.

18

CARROW

I pressed myself against the wall, silent and still, waiting.

Finally, a figure entered, the red cloak brilliant in the light. Coraline was fast, as if she'd been waiting for this moment a long time. She grabbed the figure and yanked it to her. He struggled, the hood falling back to reveal a squashed-looking face and black eyes.

Coraline sliced the dagger across his throat. Blood spurted, and she grinned with delight.

He slumped, but she kept the body clutched to her as she met my gaze. "We need to find a place to hide the body."

I looked out into the hall, spotting a small door across the way. I darted across the empty hall and peeked into the room. It was small and dark. Empty. I turned back to Coraline. "This should do."

We dragged the body in, then I tore off a piece of the red robe and did my best to wipe up the blood we'd spilled. It wasn't a perfect job, but it was close enough. I tossed the dirty rag into the room with the body, then shut the door.

Coraline dusted off her hands. "One down, ninety-nine to go."

"You look like you want to do them all yourself."

"I wouldn't hate it." Her lip twisted in a grimace. "I'm not normally so bloodthirsty, but after seeing what those bastards plan . . . I'll kill each of them with my bare hands if I have to."

We started down the hall, and I asked. "What *do* they plan? Beside raising Anat."

"That's enough. It's the version of Anat they want to raise that scares the crap out of me. Violent and vicious, she'll see that war breaks out over the entirety of the Earth."

I shuddered.

We passed a huge room, and something called to me, so strong I couldn't resist. I stopped to peer in through the enormous doorway.

Awe filled me at the sight of the huge space dotted with columns and the giant statue of a woman. She held an ax and wore a broken crown. It was one of the Egyptian style ones I'd seen in illustrations—the kinds the Pharaohs wore, with two prongs, one on either side. One was broken off, however, the stone paler where it had been snapped away. The damage looked recent.

Anat.

She had been calling to me all along. All throughout this. Those crazy red and white visions were from her, but why?

"It's the main temple," Coraline said. "The rest of the rooms are like administrative spaces or something."

The air felt weird—slimy, almost. Unbalanced, somehow. As if there were a constant draft sloping downward, giving the perception that the floor was tilted. It was incredibly strange, and strong enough to give me a sense of vertigo.

"There's something wrong with that room," I muttered. "With that statue."

"It's the cult's influence, I think. All of them feel like that, and it's spreading to the building itself."

I caught the sound of approaching footsteps echoing from the other side of the large room. Coraline's eyes brightened, and she perked up like a cat who'd heard the tuna can opening.

I dragged her away, vowing to return to the statue that called to me. "We can't afford a fight that will alert more people. We need to keep looking for the lever."

She nodded. "You're right."

As we hurried through the halls and rooms, darting into hiding spots anytime we heard footsteps, my hope began to dwindle. Where the hell was this damned lever?

I pressed my fingertips to my comms charm, hoping I could get in touch with anyone. There was only silence, however. Did that mean they weren't here? Or perhaps the signal was blocked by the protective dome.

A moment later, two red cloaks entered the room. Fear sliced through me, and I lunged for one, dagger already gripped in my hand. They were both about my size. Women, maybe. Not that it mattered.

I lunged, swiping out with my blade, and delivering a deep cut to the figure's chest. A small fist swiped out, nailing me across the cheek. The blow was so strong that I spun away, pain flaring.

To my left, Coraline moved like a whirlwind, slicing the other person's neck in the same maneuver she'd used earlier.

My attacker lunged for me, and I ducked low, plunging the dagger up into their gut. A groan of pain escaped their lips. I yanked the dagger free, but before I could attack, a blade appeared at the figure's throat, slicing across. I darted as blood sprayed. It hit me in the cheek, warm and wet.

I gagged.

"Sorry," Coraline whispered.

Both cloaked figures were slumped on the ground, and I dragged my shirt across my face, wiping the blood away. The hoods had fallen back to reveal two women, both pale skinned and fair haired. They had tattoos on their necks, just like our prisoner had had.

"We need to get rid of them." I looked around, hoping to find another convenient room.

There were none.

"Damn it." I scowled.

"Let's just leave them. We've already covered more than half the temple by my estimate. We're sure to find the lever soon."

I didn't like the plan but couldn't think of a better one. We stepped over the bodies and hurried away, fast and silent.

Finally, while hiding behind a door to peer into a large, nearly empty room, we found the lever. The ornate brass handle was four feet long, set into a stone base and guarded by a red cloak.

"He's asleep." Disgust and delight echoed in Coraline's voice.

But she was right.

The guard was sitting slumped against the wall, head bowed. I could hear his snores from over here.

"Normally I'd say that killing a sleeping man is unsporting," Coraline whispered. "Not today."

Before I could respond, she was darting across the hall, dagger drawn. The job was done in seconds, her blade flashing across the neck. Blood spurted, and I felt my stomach turn slightly.

This was more killing than I was used to. I knew

without a doubt that these people were the evilest of evil, with plans that could bring about the destruction of so many innocent lives.

But still . . . it was hard to give up on my human ideals and everything I'd learned at police college. Everything I'd grown up to believe.

There were certainly no juries in the magical world. Or, if there were, I hadn't seen any. And I doubted that any of the red-cloaked individuals in this cult were going to ever see any either.

"Let's do this thing," Coraline whispered from across the room.

I sprinted to her and grabbed the lever. She joined me, and together, we pulled hard on the metal rod. It resisted at first, finally giving way with a creak.

Magic exploded all around us, lights cracking and popping as the sound of shattering glass filled the air. A cold breeze rushed over me, followed by the warm heat of the sea air. The sounds of night insects filled the space.

"We did it." Coraline grinned widely.

I ran to a small square window and looked out, searching the courtyard for my friends.

No one was there. But then, I hadn't told them where to hide. They could be anywhere.

I turned to Coraline. "You need to get out of here."

"No. Someone needs to stay here and make sure the

switch isn't flipped back." Conviction gleamed in her eyes. "I'm going to do that."

"Thank you."

She nodded. "What about you?"

"I want to go back to the temple room. There was something off there. Something important."

"When I'm done, I'll come find you."

"Good luck." I hugged her tight, and she gripped me back.

I raced away from her and the lever, pressing my fingertips to my comms charm as I ran. It crackled to life, and gratitude swelled through me. "Eve? You there?"

"We're here! Did the barrier just fall? Everything looks different."

"Yeah. There are over a dozen prisoners. Cordelia is helping them escape. More than a hundred red cloaks, too."

"Shit."

"I'll be in the huge temple room with the statue. Good luck."

"Be safe."

"You, too." I thought of Grey, wishing I could see him. But now wasn't the time. *Never* was the time, in fact.

As I ran through the halls, the sound of battle began to ring around me. Lightning struck, no doubt from Eve, and the crash of magic reverberated through the air.

Screams and shouts sounded, along with the maniacal laughter of the witches as they attacked.

The battle was in full force now, but it was the statue of Anat that drew me to her. I had to get closer, had to figure out what was going on there.

I sprinted into an empty room, nearly at the statue. Only a couple rooms away, now.

"Hey!" A loud voice sounded from behind, and I whirled.

A figure staggered toward me, tall and strong. Blood poured from the throat where a wound gaped. The hood had been pulled back, revealing the memorable squashed face and black eyes of the first man that Coraline had killed with such glee.

Shock raced through me. "You should be dead."

He laughed, an ugly sound. "Never."

Shit, shit, shit.

He had *definitely* been dead. I'd seen it with my own eyes, and there was no way to survive the deep wound in his throat. Yet he was definitely walking around and ready to rip my head off.

As he neared, I felt the same dark magic that had wafted from the statue of Anat. It was slimy and unbalanced.

"What magic is this?" I demanded, dancing out of his way as I kept my dagger at the ready.

How was I supposed to kill someone who was already dead?

"The power of Anat, a gift to us." His words were a growl.

"Stolen, I am sure." I eyed him, debating where to stab or slice.

A creaking sounded from above, and I glanced up.

A huge metal chandelier hung above us, a massive, rustic thing. Cordelia sat on top of it, her little hands gripping the chain that affixed it to the ceiling.

Get out of the way, dummy.

I darted backward, and magic flashed around her hands. The chain snapped, and the light fixture came crashing down. It slammed onto the man, crushing him into the ground. He lay still.

Cordelia jumped down and dusted off her hands. *You're welcome.*

"You're getting two kebabs for that. How are the prisoners?"

Most free, our friends are working to release the rest.

"And Grey?"

Fighting like a demon to find you.

"You didn't tell him where I am?"

He won't stop to listen. He's gone crazy with worry.

The idea pulled at my heart, but I shoved the thought away. "I need to get to the statue of Anat. Go warn people that these bastards can't be killed. Maybe we need to burn them to dust."

She nodded, then darted off.

I followed, sprinting through the hall as I touched

my comms charm and warned Eve about the deathless state of our enemy.

Finally, I reached the huge room with the statue of Anat. It pulled at me, stronger than ever. The sound of battle echoed closer, and I could catch glimpses of fighting through doorways leading off the main temple room. It hadn't arrived here yet, but it would be here soon.

I sprinted across the empty space, drawn to the huge statue. As I neared it, I called upon my magic, praying I could read what I needed from the cold stone.

I skidded to a halt in front of it and slammed a hand onto the base, looking up at the towering figure of Anat.

Light flashed, and the ether sucked me in.

19

GREY

Fear iced my skin as I tore the head off one of the red cloaks standing between me and a cell containing a middle-aged woman with brilliant red hair.

Where was Carrow?

The need to find her raged through me, a beast with vicious claws and fangs. But the red cloaks had discovered us freeing the rest of the prisoners, and they'd come to stop us. If we didn't get these people out of here, the red cloaks would kill them.

Carrow would never forgive me for letting that happen.

I flung the headless body away and yanked on the door that trapped the woman. It broke away, and I flung it aside. She raced out, eyes wild and dress ragged.

"Go right," I said. "There's an exit."

"Hell no. I'm going to kill those bastards." Anger gleamed in her eyes.

Not a single prisoner had run for it so far, all opting to join the fight.

"Go right anyway. Your magic will start working again when you're out of this hallway."

"Thank you." She sprinted away.

I spun, searching for more doors. Down the way, Quinn ripped a door off its hinges, and Mac poured a potion onto a lock to break it.

"We've nearly got them all," she shouted. "Cordelia already released most."

The little raccoon had vanished recently, which meant that Carrow was in trouble. It was the only reason she'd have left the job of freeing the prisoners.

The rest of the group appeared to have things under control, and I could no longer fight my desperate desire to find Carrow.

I raced from the hall, heart pounding. The main passage outside of the dungeons was full of red cloaks. Half of them poured blood from grievous wounds. They shouldn't be able to stay upright, but their abilities defied the laws of nature.

I reached for one and tore his head off, viciousness surging through me. Blood spurted, coating my arm and shoulder, but I didn't care. I tossed the two pieces away like the refuse they were and went for another. I had no idea if they could rise again without their heads, but it was worth a shot.

I moved quickly, embracing my vampire speed as I searched for Carrow. All around, battle raged. The witches shot colorful bursts of magic—green banshee blasts, blue stunner spells, pink pain shockers.

Overhead, the ceiling was partially transparent like the rest of the temple. Lightning struck from the sky; Eve sending blasts down at the cult members as they attacked.

There was so much chaos and bloodshed that it felt like Anat had achieved her will, after all.

No.

We would stop this. We had to.

Finished with the red cloaks, I sprinted away, drawn by Carrow. I could almost feel her, that pull that was so uniquely her. Though our bond was still broken, the memories that had returned strengthened our connection.

Finally, I sprinted into an enormous room with a tall statue on one side. At its base, a golden-haired woman pressed her hand to the statue.

"Carrow!" I shouted her name just as she disappeared.

Gone.

~

Carrow

The ether spun me through space and spat me out in an eerily empty field. Smoke crawled along the ground, and a diffuse light emanated from the sky. It was dusk here, the dim light creepy as it illuminated several skeletal trees.

A shiver raced down my spine as I spun.

"Hello?" Where the hell was I?

Behind me, I spotted a woman. She was about fifty yards away, walking closer with a graceful, powerful stride. Her form flickered, alternately covered in blood, or dressed in pure white robes. The robed version of her was beautiful—shockingly so.

The bloody version of her . . .

That was terrifying. Her long dark hair was replaced by a matted, crimson mess, and her body—entirely naked—was coated in slick, red blood.

Smoke rolled along the ground in front of her, bringing with it the sound of war and an adrenaline rush that made me shake. Terror shot through me, followed by calm. The feelings alternated, so fast that it made my stomach turn. I nearly fell to my knees and vomited.

It felt just like the visions I'd had, only stronger.

I forced myself to stay upright.

As she approached, I realized that she spent more time in her gruesome form, the beautiful white-robed woman rarely appearing.

Shit. That couldn't be good.

She was only ten feet away, so close that her power felt like it could crush me from all around. I bowed, instinct driving me. "Goddess Anat."

She inspected me for a long moment, her form temporarily beautiful and clean, white robe gleaming. "Finally, you've come to end this farce."

Thunder echoed in her voice, making my bones shake. "Farce?"

"The people who have taken my will and twisted it"

Thank fates, maybe she would be reasonable. "I'm here to stop them."

"Good." Her form flickered red, and she lunged for me, claws outstretched.

I darted back, fear shooting through me. Her claws swiped across my chest, and pain flared. Blood poured down my shirt, and I gasped. Anat hissed, fangs protruding as she reached for me again. Terror drove me, and I stumbled back, out of her grip.

Her form flickered again, and the beautiful goddess reappeared, the blood gone. She looked at me with vague irritation. "You need to be faster. With the cult in residence in my temple, my dark side is more powerful than it should be. That is why I called to you. Only you can stop this."

"You were the voice in my head?"

"*Both* voices—my dark side and my light. The dark side wanted you for the same reason the cult does. If they force you to complete the ritual, I will rise again—death and destruction made form, and the entire earth will fall. The light side of me—the person I am this moment—knows that only you can stop this."

"Why me?"

"Fate. Your power is growing, but even I don't know what you really are. But you were the one that I could reach, and you are brave and strong enough to stop this."

"How do I stop them?"

"They've cast a spell and are siphoning my magic from this temple to fuel their miserable lives. They do not die, even once they are grievously injured."

"I've seen that."

"You must break the spell they have cast on my statue, which is a conduit for my power. They've desecrated my crown, which represents both sides of me. The left side is peace, the right side is war."

"They tore off the left side of the crown. I saw it."

"Yes. Find that piece of the crown and return it. You must also destroy the spell they have etched into the ground at my temple. Tear up the floor if you must.

When their spell is destroyed, they will fall without my magic to sustain them."

"Destroy your temple?"

"I can repair it."

"Then I can stop the red cloaks."

"Go." She flicked her hand, and the ether pulled me in. The last thing I saw was Anat, her form turning red once again. Then I was spinning through space.

A moment later, it spat me out in the large temple room. The sounds of battle raged, and I spun around.

Grey stood right in front of me, face white and eyes dark with worry.

"Carrow." He pulled me to him, hugging me hard.

My heart swelled, threatening to beat its way out of my chest. Thank God he was there. Thank God he was whole. So much emotion filled me that I thought I would burst. This depth of feeling would be a problem for later. For now, I didn't fight it. I hugged him tight, then pulled back.

"Where did you go?" he demanded.

Blasts of magic exploded behind him, colorful and terrifying. I'd never seen so much all at once. It was like standing in the middle of a war zone.

"I saw Anat. We can stop them by repairing the crown on her statue and destroying the dark red lines on the floor."

His gaze flicked to the statue, understanding dawning. Then he looked at the floor, where a dark red line was painted into the ground. Magic radiated from it, sparking against my calf.

"Destroy the lines?" he asked.

"Tear up the floor if you have to, but we need to break the spell that is feeding her power into the cult members. It's what keeps them alive even after their throats have been slit."

He nodded. "I'll deal with the lines. The witches can help."

I nodded. "Be careful."

He gave me one long look, his eyes sparking with something I couldn't quite identify, then sprinted away.

I pressed my hand to my comms charm. "Eve? We need to find a broken bit of stone that was once part of Anat's crown."

"On it."

I looked up, spotting her darting low to look at the crown then off across the sky.

All around, the battle raged. I slipped away, leaving the witches and my friends to keep the cult occupied. My lungs burned as I sprinted through the temple, searching for a broken bit of stone. It was a distinct shape, but how the hell were we going to find the things in a city this big?

Ten minutes later, when panic was starting to rise, Eve's voice echoed out of my comms charm. "I think I've found something. Meet me at the statue."

I spun around and raced back to the main room.

The halls were full of fighters, witches against red cloaks. The witches were tearing up the ground, using their magic to gouge the stone and destroy the red line. I prayed that we were only destroying the magical shadow of the temple and not the ancient floor itself.

The red cloaks tried to stop the witches, and the fighting was fierce. I dodged blasts of magic that exploded all around, ducking under the flying fists of red cloaks who sought to block my way.

As I sprinted back into the main temple room, I spotted the torn-up floor around the red line. Grey had done his part. Now Eve and I had to do ours.

"Up here," Eve shouted from above.

I looked up, spotting her. She darted down into the room, forcing her way through the semi-transparent roof. A huge piece of stone was clutched in her hands.

"That's it!" I grabbed it from her, inspecting the shape.

One of the red cloaks roared, then another. They'd spotted me holding the piece of Anat's statue, and rage echoed in their voices. They sprinted for me. Eve turned toward them, shooting lighting from her palms.

"Go," she shouted. "I'll cover you!"

I tucked the broken piece of stone under my arm like an American football and ran toward the statue. It soared thirty feet overhead. How the hell was I going to climb it with this thing in my arms?

As if she'd heard my worry, Mac appeared at my side, shoving her brown shoulder bag at me. "Here!"

"Thanks!" I shoved the stone into the bag, looped it over my back, then began to climb the statue.

It was rough going, the stone smooth and slick. I found handholds in the dress and kept climbing. All around, the sounds of battle raged. Out of the corner of my eye, I caught sight of more red cloaks converging. Most were bloodied and beaten. They should be dead.

My friends fought them, trying to buy me time as I climbed. Quinn had adopted his panther form, and he tore into the red cloaks viciously. Mac threw potion bombs with deadly accuracy and Eve shot lighting. Seraphia worked steadily in the background, destroying the red line painted into the ground with a pickax that someone must have conjured for her. The witches formed a barricade between me and the attackers.

But the red cloaks were so powerful. They shot massive blasts of magic at my friends, concussive booms that bowled over witches like bowling pins.

I climbed faster, my muscles burning. Finally, I reached the top. I stood on her shoulder as I tugged the bag around to my front.

Weak, I leaned against Anat's head, my body trembling from the magic that pulsed out of her crown. It felt as powerful as she had felt, and it was all bad feelings. Rage and despair and violence. Her warlike side.

I prayed that magic would adhere the broken piece

of the crown to the statue, because I had no mortar or glue. I pulled the broken piece of the statue out of the bag and raised it with trembling arms.

Down below, a shout caught my attention.

It was a roar of rage. Of terror.

I glanced down just in time to see a red cloak at the base of the statue. His hands were raised, glowing a violent green.

I'd seen that green before.

The sorcerers had hurled a blast like that at Grey, and it had nearly killed him. *This,* however, was far bigger. Far more powerful. I could feel it from there. If that hit me, it would kill me in an instant.

But Grey had seen it, too. He stood at the base of the statue, guarding me. The red cloak was right below him, aiming for me. Magic pulsed as he flung his hands upward, throwing the blast of deadly power right at me.

Grey leapt, putting himself between me and the blast, taking the hit straight on and landing on top of the red cloak.

He lay still.

Terror surged through me, fear like I'd never known. But the stone was heavy in my hand, and the battle raged on. Only I could stop it.

Worried tears pricked my eyes as I raised the stone to the crown, pressing it to the broken section. Panic threatened to eat me whole as magic flared. Like a cool breeze, it whispered through the room. The painted lines in the floor faded, no longer able to conduct Anat's magic.

One by one, it washed over the red cloaks. They dropped like flies, their bodies turning to dust as their cloaks puddled on the ground. The sound of battle faded.

Frantic, I scrambled down the statue, desperate to get to Grey. As I neared him, I felt it.

The bond.

It surged back into me, our mate bond, so powerful that I nearly collapsed.

Whatever he'd done, he'd reestablished the bond. Tears streamed down my face as I fell the final few feet, landing in a pile at his side.

He lay crumpled on top of the red fabric that had once outfitted a cult member. That bastard had turned to dust, however.

"Grey!" I pulled him over, running my hands over his body and reaching for the pulse at his neck. "Grey! Wake up."

Tears blurred my vision as I pressed my fingertips to his neck, feeling for a pulse.

Figures fell to their knees beside me, but I paid them no attention. I didn't even know who they were. I didn't care.

Finally, I found a pulse. Faint and weak, but there.

I dragged my sleeve over my eyes, wiping away tears

and clearing my vision. Grey looked even worse than I'd feared.

His face was so pale he looked dead, and his eyes were closed. Deep shadows hollowed out his face, tearing a hole in my chest.

I looked up. "Someone help him. A healer. Something."

One of the witches rested her hands on him, a frown stretching across her face. "He's nearly dead."

"But not totally. Save him."

Her gaze flickered up to mine, worry in their depths. "I'll do what I can, but . . ."

"Just do it." I gripped his hand, fear and hope crashing around inside me. Our bond roared, the mate connection stronger than ever.

Cursed Mate.

That would be back too, but I'd deal with it when Grey was well.

The unknown witch pressed her hands to his chest. Several more witches beat their way to the front, shoving aside their coven members.

"Non-healers clear out," Beth shouted.

They did as they were commanded, and more women joined us, pressing their palms flat to Grey. Healing magic glowed golden from their palms, flowing into him.

Seraphia joined us, keeping her eyes on Grey. She rested her palm on his forehead, and tiny green plants sprouted up through the broken stone. They leaned toward Grey, seeming to transfer magic from themselves and into him.

I looked up at Seraphia, but she didn't meet my gaze.

The room was silent as the healers worked. In the distance, I spotted more of them tending to their friends. Grey wasn't the only one wounded, but he was the worst off.

Every second was an eternity. I wanted to scream my rage and worry to the sky, but I swallowed it down.

Finally, he moved.

His eyes opened.

The witches moved back.

"Grey?" Hope flared in my chest. "Are you all right?"

"I'm—" He sat up, rubbing his face. "I'm fine."

The witches climbed to their feet and melted away. Seraphia disappeared like a ghost. But I only had eyes for Grey. I flung my arms around him, hugging him close. His arms, warm and strong, wrapped around me.

He crushed his mouth to mine, kissing me like he would never let me go. Connection and joy and comfort surged through me, like coming home.

I couldn't get enough. I wanted to absorb him into me until our two souls became one. It took everything I had to tear myself away.

His gaze searched mine, worried and beautiful.

Everything felt right when we were like this. As if the

earth were finally turning on a proper axis after millennia of being off kilter.

Now that our bond was back, I realized I'd been walking around feeling like I was missing a limb.

And yet . . .

We were still Cursed Mates.

EPILOGUE

CARROW

The next day, I stood in the Shadow Guild tower, covered in dust as I tried to scrub out the ghosts that still haunted the place. The last twenty-four hours had been a whirlwind.

After the battle, the Temple of Anat had begun to repair itself almost immediately, magic flowing out from the statue of Anat to mend the floors and remove the red paint that the cult members had applied. Once the crown had been repaired, she must have regained her power.

We'd lost none of our forces, though there had been some truly gruesome injuries that would take time to heal, even with magic. All of the kidnap victims were home, thank God.

Grey and I had parted almost immediately. The kiss had ended, and we'd realized we shouldn't be around each other. We were still cursed mates. All our work to break the mate bond was undone.

My theory was that Grey's act of sacrifice to save me must have broken it. He'd thrown himself into that blast without hesitating.

But now what?

Even though the bond had been broken, I'd fallen for him even harder. I wanted to be with him, with or without the bond.

I scrubbed a hand over my face, head pounding. I'd come to the Guild Tower to think about it all—to try to figure a way out of the future that was barreling toward us—but I was no closer to an answer.

"You want a drink or something?" Mac asked from my side.

I blinked, startled, and looked up at her. I'd totally forgotten she was there. "What?"

"A drink? Or a break? You look like you need one."

I dragged a weary hand through my dusty hair. "I could probably use one, yeah. It's been a long week."

"It's not that."

I shook my head. "Fine. You see right through me. It's Grey."

"What are you going to do?"

"I don't know. What *is* there to do?" Memories of how wasted away he'd looked after his disappearance flashed into my mind. It hadn't taken long for the curse to wear him down. "If he doesn't kill me, he'll waste away. Quickly."

"Well, he's not going to kill you."

"If he can help it. He'd said he couldn't control it when he was too far gone."

She grimaced. "Yeah, that's bad."

I turned back to the piles of boxes in front of me. All were made of wood; most were nailed shut. They called to me, making my fingers itch to open them.

For some weird reason, I felt there were answers here. About what, I wasn't sure. About me? About Grey? About Rasla, who I was still obsessed with? Why had he hated the Shadow Guild so much? What was it about those who were different?

Maybe there were answers to everything here. Or maybe it was desperation. Because I *was* desperate now. I didn't know if I loved Grey, but I certainly didn't want to lose him. And I didn't want to lose my life. But unless I figured something out, that was going to happen.

No.

I could do this. I'd gotten myself out of miserable scrapes before, and I was going to get myself out of this.

"Come on," I said to Mac. "Let's look through these boxes. There's got to be something good in them."

. . .

~~~

Cursed Mate, the final book in Carrow and Grey's, series will be available at the end of August, 2020. Check it out on Amazon.

THANK YOU!

THANK YOU FOR READING!

I hope you enjoyed reading this book as much as I enjoyed writing it. Reviews are *so* helpful to authors. I really appreciate all reviews, both positive and negative. If you want to leave one, you can do so at Amazon or GoodReads.

ACKNOWLEDGMENTS

Thank you, Ben, for everything. There would be no books without you.

Thank you to Jena O'Connor, Lexi George, and Ash Fitzsimmons for your excellent editing. The book is immensely better because of you! Thank you to Susie for your incredibly keen eye on typos.

Thank you to Orina Kafe for the beautiful cover art.

AUTHOR'S NOTE

Thank you so much for reading *Devilish Game*! As always, there were a few historical tidbits that I wanted to share more about. The most obvious one is the ancient city of Ugarit. It is an archaeological site located near the Mediterranean in Syria.

The city is in ruins because it is so ancient. The tunnel that Carrow and her friends used to enter the city still remains, but the rest of the buildings are destroyed down to the lower walls. It was difficult to recreate what Ugarit would have looked like as I do not have much familiarity with that period of history. An article written by Tarek Teba and Dimitris Theodossopoulos was extremely helpful (*A Graphic Reconstruction Methodology For The Conservation of Cultural Heritage*). The tavern and plaza that featured in the scene were part of their research.

The city contains two temples—one to the god Baal and the other to the god El. El was a Semitic deity in Mesopotamia and the Near East. However, the goddess Anat suited the story better and so I replaced his temple with hers. She was roughly as I depicted her, a goddess of both war and peace.

Anat was popular in many places—from Ugarit and Egypt to Meopotamia and Israel. She was slightly different in each place, but the Atef crown that she wore in the final scene of the book was inspired by a bronze figurine found of her in Syria.

This book was dedicated to the students who are missing school during the Covid-19 crisis. My heart hurts for those who are missing school and their friends. The college party scene at the Witches' Guild came about because I was remembering how much fun I had in college (at parties like the one I described, except without the random and ridiculous array of football fight songs).

That's it for the historical elements in the book. There will be one more in Carrow and Grey's series, and I hope you will come back to read it!

ABOUT LINSEY

Before becoming a writer, Linsey Hall was a nautical archaeologist who studied shipwrecks from Hawaii and the Yukon to the UK and the Mediterranean. She credits fantasy and historical romances with her love of history and her career as an archaeologist. After a decade of tromping around the globe in search of old bits of stuff that people left lying about, she settled down and started penning her own romance novels. Her Dragon's Gift series draws upon her love of history and the paranormal elements that she can't help but include.

COPYRIGHT

www.LinseyHall.com
https://www.facebook.com/LinseyHallAuthor

Made in the USA
Middletown, DE
13 November 2020